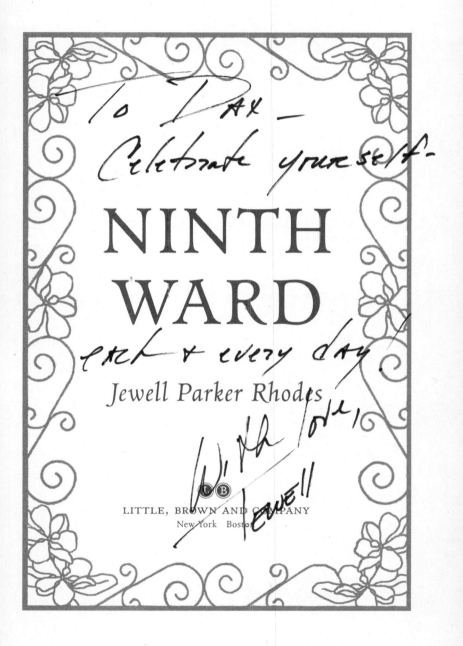

To Dax —
Celebrate yourself —

NINTH WARD

each & every day!

Jewell Parker Rhodes

With love,
Jewell

LITTLE, BROWN AND COMPANY
New York   Boston

Little, Brown and Company

Hachette Book Group
237 Park Avenue, New York, NY 10017
Visit our Web site at www.lb-kids.com

Little, Brown and Company is a division of Hachette Book Group, Inc.
The Little, Brown name and logo are trademarks of Hachette Book Group, Inc.

First Edition: August 2010

The characters and events portrayed in this book are fictitious. Any similarity to real persons, living or dead, is coincidental and not intended by the author.

Library of Congress Cataloging-in-Publication Data
Rhodes, Jewell Parker.
    Ninth Ward / by Jewell Parker Rhodes. —1st ed.
        p. cm.
    Summary: In New Orleans's Ninth Ward, twelve-year-old Lanesha, who can see spirits, and her adopted grandmother have no choice but to stay and weather the storm as Hurricane Katrina bears down upon them.
    ISBN 978-0-316-04307-6
    1. Hurricane Katrina, 2005—Juvenile fiction. [1. Hurricane Katrina, 2005—Fiction. 2. Spirits—Fiction. 3. Coming of age—Fiction. 4. Survival—Fiction. 5. African Americans—Fiction. 6. New Orleans (La.)—Fiction.] I. Title.
    PZ7.R3476235Ni 2010
    [Fic]—dc22   2009034423

10 9 8 7 6 5

Book design by Alison Impey

RRD-C

Printed in the United States of America

Dedicated to all the children
who experienced Hurricane Katrina
and the levees breaking in New Orleans

Sunday

They say I was born with a caul, a skin netting covering my face like a glove. My mother died birthing me. I would've died, too, if Mama Ya-Ya hadn't sliced the bloody membrane from my face. I let out a wail when she parted the caul, letting in first air, first light.

Every year on my birthday, Mama Ya-Ya tells me the same story. "Lanesha, your eyes were the lightest green. With the tiniest specks of yellow. With them eyes, and that caul, I knew you'd have the *sight*."

Mama Ya-Ya smacks her lips and laughs. Afterwards, we always have cake. Chocolate. Today, I'm twelve. I've eaten three pieces of cake.

∽

Mama Ya-Ya's eighty-two. Half blind now, she's still raising me 'cause my relatives won't. I have a whole family full of uncles, aunts, cousins, nieces, grandmothers, and whatnot. They live in Uptown. Richer than where I live, the Ninth Ward, New Orleans. Less than eight miles apart. It might as well be the moon. Or Timbuktu, wherever that is.

Mama Ya-Ya says my family is scared of me. "Everybody in Louisiana knows there be spirits walking this earth. All kinds of ghosts you can't see, not unless they want you to. But you, child, you see them. You've got the *sight*. It's grace to see both worlds," she says as we wash our birthday dishes, sticky with bits of jambalaya.

"Better you be an orphan, your family thinks.

Better crazy Mama Ya-Ya raises you," she says, sucking air through her false teeth. "Fine. I'm old school. Don't care nothin' about folks who dishonor traditions as old as Africa. I'll be your mother and grandmother both."

And she is. I love her more than anything in this whole wide world.

⌒〜◯

I love saying "Mama Ya-Ya." Her name sounds so bright and happy, just like Mama Ya-Ya is.

And I love how Mama Ya-Ya says my name—"*Lanesha.*" Soft, with the *ah* sound going on forever.

Lanesha—that's the name my mother gave me. Last word she said before she died. I don't remember hearing it. But I imagine she said it then just like Mama Ya-Ya does now.

Upstairs, I sometimes see my mother's ghost on Mama Ya-Ya's bed, her belly big, like she's forgotten she already gave birth to me.

Like she's stuck and can't move on. Like she forgot I was already born.

Just like my Uptown relatives forgot today was my birthday. They always forget.

∽

Me and Mama Ya-Ya wrap the leftover cake in foil. Mama Ya-Ya shuffles towards the living room. I follow her like a shadow. We have been together all day long.

Gardening, we cut sunflowers for the kitchen table. We chopped ham and onions for the jambalaya; then we played cards while the rice cooked. I squeezed lemons for lemonade while Mama Ya-Ya frosted the cake. A perfect day.

I say, "I wish I could see my father. Dead or alive, don't matter."

"Lanesha, I don't know who he is. Or where he is. Or if he still is. Your momma died before she could say. Maybe she didn't want to say. Don't know. She weren't but seventeen. One of them beautiful, light-skinned Fontaine girls. Proud of their French heritage. Uptown's finest to be sure.

"I think your momma fell in love with a Ninth Ward boy. Rich girl, poor boy. He must've been darker, too. For you are a fine brown, Lanesha. Like pralines."

"Maybe they were secretly married like Romeo and Juliet," I say. I like the idea of my parents holding hands, being brave, and exchanging rings.

I learned about Romeo and Juliet in school. We don't have Shakespeare plays, just these little booklets that tell us about the plays. *Synopses,* my teacher calls them. I don't believe in Santa Claus anymore, but if I did, I'd ask him to bring me a whole set of Shakespeare books. The real ones, with the real words Shakespeare wrote. Then I wouldn't have to take the smelly bus to the city library.

The bus also takes me uptown, but not as far uptown as my relatives live. I think about riding further and further, walking up to their house door, and knocking, but I don't. I get scared that they may not answer.

Instead, I go to the library and try to read *The Tragedy of Romeo and Juliet*, but it's too hard. I looked up *tragedy* in my pocket dictionary. Mama Ya-Ya gave it to me for my birthday last year. **TRAGEDY:** A CHARACTER IS BROUGHT TO RUIN OR SUFFERS EXTREME SORROWS. I check out the movie *Romeo + Juliet* for me and Mama Ya-Ya to watch. Hearing the words in the movie, I still don't understand everything. But I can see Romeo and Juliet's love, see how their families fought.

The party scene is my favorite. Juliet is dressed so fine in the prettiest long, flowing gown. She wears white angel wings. Romeo wears a silver, glittering knight's suit with a sword.

They just look at each other from across the room and fall in love.

I think that's what happened to my parents, too. They must have gone to a party and while the DJ was spinning records, they fell in love. Everybody else cleared the floor, watching my folks dance fast, slow, even hip-hop.

One day, I'll be able to read all of Shakespeare's words and understand everything he's saying. Like *star-crossed*, which doesn't mean stars zigzagging across the sky. It means "doomed."

My parents were star-crossed. That's why I think my mother is still here, upstairs, a ghost in Mama Ya-Ya's bed. She's waiting for the day my dad—ghost or not—claims us both.

Once we're in the living room and Mama Ya-Ya is settled in her favorite chair—all soft with a blue lap shawl—I say, "I memorized some Shakespeare. Want to hear?"

"Course I do." She gives me her full attention.

I stand on the old living room carpet, imagining I'm onstage. My hands stretch wide, and I imagine I'm speaking to the whole world. Even if it's only Mama Ya-Ya watching me. I say, "For never was a story of more woe/Than this of Juliet and her Romeo." Then, my hands over my heart, I bow my head.

Smiling, Mama Ya-Ya claps, long and hard. "Oh, Lanesha. Your mother and father made magic when they made you."

Mama Ya-Ya sits back in her chair. Mama Ya-Ya is so tiny, and the chair almost swallows her. Her feet barely touch the floor. Her hair is silver and her skin reminds me of a walnut, all wrinkly brown. On the wall above her head is a picture of her favorite president—William Jefferson Clinton.

Mama Ya-Ya closes her eyes. She does that a lot now. She reminds me of a clock winding down. Her head tilts; her body relaxes in the chair like a balloon losing air.

I take out my birthday gift, a package of sparkly pens Mama Ya-Ya has given me. I pull out the purple ink pen and write:

Romeo + Juliet = Me

Ten times.

I like practicing cursive. It makes me feel grown.

Lanesha   Mama Ya-Ya

I like watching Mama Ya-Ya sleep. Sometimes, she twitches with dreams.

If I wanted to wake her, all I'd need to say is "Oprah" and she'd be wide-awake, hollering for her Coke-bottle glasses and for me to turn on the TV. But we've celebrated a lot today. She should rest. Every day this summer, we watched Oprah. Mama Ya-Ya says, "Oprah is a southern girl. That's why she's got so much sense!"

I like it when Oprah laughs and when she talks about love. I think she must love everybody she knows. I always wonder, if she knew me, would she love me?

This I know for certain: Mama Ya-Ya loves me as the day is long. She is the only one who loves me through and through. When I'm too dreamy, when I don't finish my chores, when I'm grumpy and sad, Mama Ya-Ya just hugs me a long time. Even when she scolds, she finishes with a hug.

When she holds me that close, I can always smell

Mama Ya-Ya's Vicks Rub and Evening in Paris perfume. Vicks Rub comes in a green bottle and smells of eucalyptus and menthol. It smells cool and tickles my nose. Evening in Paris is in a midnight blue bottle and smells warm like trees mixed with magnolias. It seems like the two would smell bad together, but they don't. No one makes Evening in Paris anymore. "Soon it'll all be used up. Like me," Mama Ya-Ya says every day, dabbing perfume behind her ears. I always shake my head.

This morning, though, Mama Ya-Ya frowned at the mirror like she could see some other world inside it. "Mr. Death is losing patience. He'll come and ferry me down the Mississippi. I'll put on my feathered hat. Wave like I'm in a Mardi Gras parade."

I don't like to hear Mama Ya-Ya talk like that.

Mama Ya-Ya's chin is on her chest. She is fast asleep, dreaming.

I put my purple pen back inside the plastic case. I stroke Mama Ya-Ya's hand. Her head lifts; her eyes flutter.

"Mama Ya-Ya, let me help you to bed," I say.

"You are a good child." She pats my cheek. "Did you have a good day? A good birthday day?"

"Yes, ma'am." It was a good day.

❧

Mama Ya-Ya leans on my right arm. Her cane is shiny ebony with an ivory skull on top. Her fingers wrap around that skull for dear life. We walk slowly — inch by inch, step by step, to her small bedroom (my mother's ghost is gone). Her bed is a high four-poster with white sheets and yellow quilt. Lace curtains hang limp over the two front windows. There isn't any breeze. Just stuffy heat and fading sun. Striped green wallpaper covers the walls.

On the nightstand is a glass for her false teeth and blood pressure pills, cod-liver oil, and rosemary leaves. She puts the rosemary in tea to calm her arthritis.

Mama Ya-Ya's altar is in the far corner. It is a small table filled with flickering candles and statues of

Catholic saints and voodoo gods. Her rosary cross is silver, with sparkling blue beads. Next to a plate offering the gods beans and rice is her black midwife bag. The bag is never opened and it never moves. But I know Mama Ya-Ya still touches her bag. She keeps it cleaned, locked with all her birthing stuff inside. Always ready.

⁓

I slip Mama Ya-Ya's black clodhopper shoes off her tiny feet.

"I should be putting you to bed," she says.

"It's my turn," I say, smiling. "'Sides, I never had a baby doll."

Mama Ya-Ya chuckles. "Are you saying I'm a baby doll?"

I burst out laughing. "No, ma'am." My cheeks are warm. The thought of Mama Ya-Ya as an overgrown doll tickles me. "Got you," I say.

"You sure did, Lanesha. Me, a baby doll. Hah!

Go on, now. I can take care of myself. Me, a baby doll." Mama Ya-Ya is puttering, taking her nightgown out the drawer and laying her glasses on the nightstand. She is grinning, muttering, "Baby doll. Big windup toy. Chatty Cathy." She is happy. Laughing.

"'Night, Mama Ya-Ya." She doesn't hear me.

I skip across the hall to my room, happy that I made Mama Ya-Ya laugh.

 ༄

I plop down on my bed. I love my room.

This summer, Mama Ya-Ya let me paint the walls different shades of blue. One wall is Robin's Egg Blue. Another, Ocean Blue. Another, Blue Sky. And the wall behind my headboard is Blueberry. I used a rolling brush and it was as easy as rolling pie dough: Back and forth. Up and down. Turn around. Roll the roller in the pan. Back and forth. Up and down. Over and over and over.

My hands were blue for a week. Pieces of my hair, too. I didn't mind.

I lie back and stretch. The ceiling is bright white, like my bedsheets and comforter. I promised Mama Ya-Ya I wouldn't get ink on the sheets or dirt on the comforter. And I haven't. It's the prettiest room in the whole house!

My room does have puzzle pictures on the wall. I like tiny puzzle pieces with colors on them. I like trying to figure out where they fit. Mama Ya-Ya and I have finished several puzzles together, and some I've done all on my own. Afterwards, I glue the pieces together and hang them on the wall. There is a puzzle picture of wild flowers — all yellow, red, orange, and white in a field. There is a picture of a monkey, too, hanging upside down from a tree. My favorite is the picture of a steamboat churning up the Mississippi. I think I'd like traveling by water. Unlike dirt, water seems alive, moving and shifting, always making lapping sounds against the boat and shore. On the right wall, above my dresser, I have a picture of the Eiffel Tower in Paris, all lit up with lights. I like it because it looks like a Christmas tree. It took me months to fit all those itty-bitty pieces of light into something beautiful.

❧

Outside, the sunset has turned from orange to purple. I still have math to finish. It's the third week of school and I want to get ahead.

I grab my math book. I love flipping through the pages. Squiggly marks everywhere. Plus, +, equal, =, less than, <, greater than, >. Alphabet letters. Numbers.

Since I was at least three, Mama Ya-Ya always said, "Signs everywhere, Lanesha. Pay attention." And I did. Do.

I learned three apples could be the number 3. In math, the apples can even be a *y* or an *x*. Squiggly marks can be *symbols*. "A sign for something that is more than it is."

If I was blind, I could even rub my fingers over dots. Braille, it's called. Raised dots, like pink candy on white sheets, can tell you what elevator button to push, or what door leads to the GIRLS' BATHROOM, or tell you a story like *The Three Little Pigs*.

My new English teacher, Miss Perry, and my math teacher, Miss Johnson, both talk about symbols.

Signs.

Romeo + Juliet

Word and math signs mixed.

But I like Mama Ya-Ya's signs best: "Ladybugs mean good luck"; "The Little Dipper means freedom. Its handle is the North Star"; "The color blue means strength and friendliness. Happiness."

Whenever Mama Ya-Ya talks about colors, she'll put her hands on her hips, cock her head, and tease, "Who loves blue in this house?"

"Me," I always say.

Doing laundry, cooking, cleaning, Mama Ya-Ya keeps teaching me every day.

"Dreaming about alligators means trouble," she said this morning. "Numbers mean something, too. Not just math, Lanesha. Three means life. Eight means power. Four means hard work in this here world. The material world. Put them together and they can mean something else." She smacks her gums. "Put 4 and 8 together and it equals 12. That's spiritual strength. Real strength, Lanesha. Some people doubt it because they can't see it on the outside. Like butterflies. To most folks, they seem delicate. But the truth is, butterflies keep changing, no matter what, going from ugly worm to hard cocoon to strong wings.

"Always look for the signs, Lanesha," she said. "Even flowers. Magnolias mean dignity. Beauty."

Magnolia trees grow all over our neighborhood. The big trees, with their buttery white petals, bloom sweet all spring.

If Mama Ya-Ya were a flower, I'm pretty sure she'd be a magnolia.

❧

I lean back into my pillows, take out the purple pen, and write in my math notebook.

Me

Lanesha

Twelve

$8 + 4 = 12$

All marks — signs — written in my best cursive.
Symbols of me.

Who cares about a stupid Uptown family?

Mama Ya-Ya + Lanesha = Love

I ♡ Me

Like a butterfly, I am strong.

Monday

I do see ghosts. Have since I was an itty-bitty baby.

Ghosts. Here, now. Always. They're soft, wispy. I can put my hand through them. If I blow hard enough, I can make them shiver.

Ghosts don't frighten me. Most of them just look lost — like they can't understand what's happened to them. Their eyes blank, their ghost bodies wander about.

When I was younger, I used to think there were just old and older ghosts. But in school, we've been studying New Orleans's history and now I can spot differences better.

Ghosts wearing yellow silk ball gowns with flowers in their hair, and waving silk fans. Cool men wearing slanted hats to make them look slick, and tapping rhythms with their brown and white suede shoes.

Ghosts wearing jeans and colored beads like they wear during Mardi Gras. They carry signs: MAKE LOVE, NOT WAR. Their fingers make a V, the peace sign.

Now, ghosts in baggy pants, their underwear showing, wearing short-sleeve T-shirts and body tattoos, are from my time. They're mostly boys killed in drive-bys or fights or robberies. Sometimes, I know them from school. Like Jermaine. One day I'm seeing him in the cafeteria eating macaroni, the next day he's a ghost, dull eyed, high-fiving me, saying, "Hey, Lanesha."

I always answer "Hey," even if he was mean to me when he was alive.

Every morning since I started my new school, Jermaine's ghost waits for me on the school steps.

He should be starting middle school with the rest of us. Instead, he sits on the steps, watching everyone pass by.

Jermaine used to skip school lots. His last skip, he was in a 7-Eleven buying a soda. He got a belly shot. Wrong place, wrong time. He never got to graduate. I always wave at him. Sometimes, he says, "You're cool, Lanesha." Other times, "Stay in school." (As if I wouldn't!) I don't remind him that he used to make fun of my green-yellow eyes, and call me "Evil Eye" or "Devil Eye," and make "OoooOooo Oooooo" scary movie sounds whenever I walked by.

Kids at school have always teased me: "Crazy Lanesha," "Spooky Lanesha," "Witch Lanesha." I just try to ignore them. They make me feel bad and sometimes I even cry. Still, I don't tell them that if they're shot dead or drowned in the swamp or smashed by a car, they'll be glad I can see them. I'll remind them of home. Of being alive.

Sometimes the teasing is just too much, though, and I go in the girls' bathroom to hide. When I'm most sad, I think of Mama Ya-Ya. I see her in my mind like she's a ghost, and it comforts me. "You are loved, Lanesha," she always says. "Lanesha, you are loved."

❦

TaShon, my neighbor from down the street, is in my English class. Every time I see TaShon, I get the feeling that we're related. After all, Mama Ya-Ya helped birth us both. Except TaShon's mother still lives. Mine died. And I was born first.

Mama Ya-Ya doesn't birth babies anymore. Everybody goes to Charity Hospital. TaShon, the last baby she birthed, was born with extra fingers. Two little bumps growing out of the sides of his hands. Mama Ya-Ya tried to tell everyone it was a good sign, saying, "He'll cling hard to life." Before TaShon was born, another baby had died. "Born premature," Mama Ya-Ya said. "Because of you," said the pitiful mother. It was easier for everyone to believe the mother. To doubt the strength of Mama Ya-Ya's roots and herbs.

Then, there'd been me. Born with a caul. The ignorant say, "Witch's spawn."

One baby dead, one born with a caul, and one trying to grow twelve fingers — it was enough for all the would-be mothers to go to Charity. No time for a midwife anymore.

When I see TaShon on our street, I wave. He's a sad boy. Picked on all the time, even though his dad sliced off the extra skin on his hands when he was born. Now he has small stumps where his extra fingers used to be. His dad works hard all day at the wharf. His momma, Mrs. Williams, cleans at the Riverwalk Casino — daytime, nighttime, overtime. "Anytime I can get," Mrs. Williams chuckles. Nights, when she isn't working, she sings gospel at the New Life Church, a few blocks over.

TaShon keeps so quiet, and I think his parents forget he's there. But I think he keeps quiet because, like a ghost, he doesn't want to be noticed. He's short. Shorter than all the sixth-grade girls. Every year, in every grade, he's been the shortest kid. Every year, in every grade, he has a far-off look. Like he doesn't see what's up close, just what's far, like treetops, or where the ground meets the sky. TaShon slides around the halls, keeps still on the school yard. The ghosts see him. I wish he could see them.

In class, TaShon doesn't look at the blackboard. Sometimes, he plays tic-tac-toe, by himself. Other times, he hums, and when the boys hear him, they sometimes smack his head. Most times, he stares out the window past the safety bars to his own world.

At school, I don't say, "Hey, TaShon," 'cause I'd only make his teasing worse. It isn't fair.

Whenever I see how sad and lonely TaShon is, it makes me doubt Mama Ya-Ya is right about him clinging hard to life. But I keep faith.

Like Mama Ya-Ya keeps faith in me.

"When the time's right," Mama Ya-Ya always says, "the universe shines down love."

❧

Mama Ya-Ya says, "There are more good signs in this world, Lanesha, than bad." In school, I think my teachers count for more goodness than a trillion kids teasing me. Even though I'm teased, my new middle school feels good. Miss Perry, my Teach for America English teacher, is wearing yellow, and yellow means peace.

"Class," she says, "today's vocabulary word is *fortitude*. 'Strength to endure.' "

I like the word. I like how when saying it, my tongue touches the top of my teeth.

I look across at TaShon. I'm surprised. He's listening to Miss Perry, too.

Maybe, like me, TaShon loves words, too. *Fortitude* is three syllables. Three is a powerful number. It means life. It means making peace with your thoughts, words, and deeds.

I can't wait to tell Mama Ya-Ya my new word.

Tuesday

The next day I keep thinking about all Mama Ya-Ya
has told me. "Signs everywhere. Pay attention."

And I do. Noticing that the flowers on the way to
school seem thirsty. Noticing that our school is old
and crumbling, but it always feels brand-new 'cause
the blackboard changes. Chalk — red, blue, white,
and green — is powerful, sending me signals.

I watch as my math teacher Miss Johnson tries to help Andrew understand *her* signs. Math signs. Miss Johnson explains again and again, ever so careful. Kind.

Andrew always gets stuck on questions like: "How come $y = x + c$? Why not z?"; "How come water boils?"; "Why didn't Lincoln play cards instead of going to see a show?" Every year we've been in school together, they pass him — even though grown-ups say he's slow. In school, he's no trouble. Folks say, "School gives his mother a babysitter so she can work." I don't believe that. Andrew is just a different smart. Like if you say, "The world is flat," Andrew's mind cuts it up into squares. Like the way my eyes see things that others swear aren't there.

Usually, I just don't say anything. I do my work and keep my head down. But today, my third day being twelve, I whisper to Andrew: "I'll help. At lunch, I'll show you why numbers and letters mean."

"Mean what?" asks Andrew.

His eyes are brown and curious. He acts as if I've

been talking to him all these years. But I haven't. Like TaShon, I don't want him to get teased more for talking to me. At my new school, I see only popular kids hang in twos and threes, or in groups. Sometimes, they all wear short black skirts, or have their hair braided with the same color beads, or laugh at kids like me, Andrew, and TaShon.

"Mean what?" asks Andrew, his finger tapping my desk.

"Quantity. Numbers are signs for how much."

Andrew smiles, polite.

The bell rings and I say, "Come on."

Our school yard is nothing but concrete with an old handball wall and fading basketball lines. Most kids stand around, looking bored. Me, I usually bring a book to keep me company. Today, I have Andrew. Andrew who usually just stays inside.

We sit at a rusty picnic table. The sun is warming us good. I glare at anyone walking by, daring them to tease us. I must have an invisible sign that says, "Don't mess with Lanesha." Because no one says nothing.

Or maybe, everyone's shocked to see Andrew outside?

"Math problems," I say.

Andrew looks at me. He has freckles on his nose. His T-shirt has a hole, and when he shifts, I can see his belly button.

Behind Andrew I see a skinny ghost with a beard and bow tie. I wonder if it's a teacher from long ago.

I draw the numbers 5 + 5 and 6 + 6 and 7 + 7. Then, I write 5 × 2, 6 × 2, 7 × 2. "Are these the same? Is 5 plus 5 the same as 2 × 5?"

Andrew blinks.

I think the problems are easy, but Andrew doesn't answer.

I try again. "Here," I say. "Count these." I draw little sticks to add up to 10.

Andrew blinks again. "I don't need math. Math doesn't need me." Then, he scoots closer, and leans in like he's going to tell me a secret. He whispers: "Do you know why there's air?"

"So you can breathe," I answer.

He nods. "So we can live," he says. "Can't see it, but

it's always here." He sucks in air, and his cheeks hollow like a skeletor.. "Inside." He points at his chest. Then, he opens his mouth wide, and blows his air out like he's pretending to be the big, bad wolf.

He grins and laughs loudly.

Me and Andrew high-five. See, Andrew's smart. Different smart.

The ghost puts up a hand for a high five, but I ignore him.

We sit, comfortable. Andrew shows me the ants crawling across the table. "Look at them breathe," he says.

I answer: "Mama Ya-Ya would like you." Then, I add, "She doesn't need math, either."

But I do, I think.

Mama Ya-Ya never went to school. Her mother taught her and her mother's mother taught her mother.

I need everything Mama Ya-Ya teaches me. And I need everything that school teaches me, too.

I need all the signs. Dreams. Words. Word problems. Math.

Like air, they make my mind breathe.

The bell rings. I pat Andrew's hand. "You're smart, Andrew."

He ducks his head like a baby bird.

"Like me!" I say.

"Like me," he crows.

We walk back to the classroom and nobody—I swear!—bothers us.

❧

After school, my teacher, Miss Johnson, teaches me. On Tuesdays, I try and stay late so we can work on harder problems.

Miss Johnson says, "Lanesha, you're like a sponge."

Sponges are ugly, but I think I know what Miss Johnson means.

I try to work hard. Mama Ya-Ya says, "Just 'cause you're smart doesn't mean everything's gonna be easy. You have to set your mind to learning, Lanesha. Each and every day."

When I can't solve a problem, I get frustrated, but

when I do solve it. I feel like singing, like I don't have any worries in the whole wide world.

"You could be an engineer," Miss Johnson says.

"Engineers build things," I say, feeling happy, strong.

"Yes."

"Like houses, apartments, and such?"

"More like dams. Bridges. Wait." She gets up, digs in her purse. "My friend sent me a postcard," she says, handing it to me.

A beautiful red bridge rises out of the mist over water.

"The Golden Gate."

"Why's it called that?"

"I don't know. You could find out. It's a suspension bridge."

"What's that mean?"

"Look it up."

"You sound like Miss Perry." I will, too. Look it up. I know what *suspense* means. But what does it mean for a bridge? What does it mean in math?

My fingers trace the bridge over the Pacific Ocean.

It's got to be the Pacific because the front of the card says "San Francisco." I stare at the photograph. My heart races, and I feel tingly inside.

The bridge is beautiful. I could do that, I think. Build bridges. I love how they look—like strong steel butterflies, soaring high. My first bridge would be from lower Ninth Ward to Uptown, New Orleans. If I built a beautiful bridge to my family, maybe they'd walk across? Or else let me?

❧

I walk home slowly from school. Miss Johnson's postcard is in my jeans back pocket. She let me have it, even though the card had writing: "Dear Evelyn, You should be here. Love, Jim."

I didn't know her name was Evelyn.

❧

The sky is bright blue like marbles with cloudy eyes. The end of summer is hurricane season, but the weather feels just fine. It is like that some-times — calm, then rains hit. I stop and smell. I smell fish, brine from the Gulf, algae from the Mis-sissippi, and somebody frying catfish. I smell some-thing else — old, sorrowful. I don't know what it is — I must ask Mama Ya-Ya. She says, "Senses tell you everything. See, touch, smell, feel. Trust your senses and you'll never lose your way."

Only difference is Mama Ya-Ya's lived a long time. Her senses have told her so much and I know so lit-tle. I'm only twelve and still have a lot to learn.

❧

I keep walking. Sniffing the air. Imagining bridges in the sky. I can already picture metal and wires, mak-ing marks, shapes against the sky. I think fitting the pieces together would be just like a jigsaw puzzle, except it wouldn't be cardboard pasted together and hung on a wall. It'd be useful with patterns, shapes that did something — helped people and cars cross the street, over water, or a deep hole in the ground.

Making bridges would be magic. Math would be my special trick. I'd only make beautiful bridges, I think, strong and as delicate as butterflies.

❧

I hear cursing, and crying.

"Hey," I shout. Some boys are dragging someone into the alley. Taunting, kicking. Punching.

A dog barks.

I hear: "Stop it."

I hate bullies.

"Hey." I push at one boy. He turns, but when he sees it's me, he doesn't hit. I am Mama Ya-Ya's crazy girl.

"What y'all doing?" I know these boys — Eddie, Max, Lavon.

"Mind your own business," says Max. He puffs out his chest, acting tough. He has always been a thug. I go toe-to-toe. I puff my chest out, too. I still don't see who they've been picking on. I keep my eyes focused on Max.

"You want to fight me," I say. No boy likes to be

dared by a girl. If he takes me up on it, I'm dead. I hear crying and I know whoever they've been picking on is gonna be no help.

"Why would I fight a girl? Waste of time."

"Yeah," says Eddie. Max scowls at him to shut up.

Max hasn't moved and his black eyes look me over. "Go home, Lanesha," Max says. "It ain't Halloween."

Eddie and Lavon coo, cackle with laughter. Max is giving high fives.

"Your momma," I say. Everyone goes quiet. Max looks fierce. Like he wants to punch me.

"Say it," I say. Max is supposed to say, "Your momma," back. But no one messes with Mama Ya-Ya. She may cast a spell on him. Of course, she'd do no such thing. She doesn't do spells. Wouldn't hurt a bug. But Max doesn't know that.

"You have skinny legs, skinny butt, skinny everything," he says. "No wonder no boy likes you. You ugly." He stretches out *uhhh-glee* like a moan. I don't mind; it's part of the game. Max keeps a little pride, and I get what I want.

I turn my back and look to see who's been picked

on. TaShon! His eye is swollen and he has his arms wrapped about a dirty dog.

"Go on," I say to Max, Eddie, and Lavon. "Pick on someone else."

"They was kicking the dog," screams TaShon. "Dog didn't hurt nobody."

Kids, at school, whisper Max once set a cat on fire.

"You're just a girl. Not worth my time."

I ball my fist. "And you're just stupid, dumber than a rock." I want Max to fight me.

"Go on, hit her," says Lavon.

"Yeah," says Eddie, his eyes bugging out like a balloon.

Max blinks. His eyes are superblack. Mean.

"Come on," Max says. "Waste of time." Him, Eddie, and Lavon walk away, trying to be cool.

I can finally breathe.

"Thanks," says TaShon. He pats the dog and the dog licks him. It's the first time I've seen TaShon smile. A big wide smile that shows his teeth!

The dog looks at me, its tongue lolling. It's a mess, matted hair — more black than brown — big paws, but its body is still small. It's still a pup, with bulging brown eyes and short, rangy hair.

TaShon is loving the dog like there's no tomorrow.

"He tried to save me, did you see?"

"He should've stopped you from getting that black eye, then. What is it? Some kind of lab-terrier mix?"

"German shepherd," says TaShon, defiant.

I think, No way, but let it pass. "Come let Mama Ya-Ya fix your eye."

"I've got to get home. Start the rice."

TaShon's mother gets home at six.

"Later," I say.

"Can you keep Spot for a while?"

"Who?" I say.

"Spot. My dog."

"Your dog doesn't have any spots."

"So? Please, Lanesha. Can you keep him? My momma won't let me keep him. 'Another mouth to feed,' she'll say." This is the most I've ever heard TaShon say!

"Well, how did you find him?"

"He found me. See," says TaShon, grinning, getting up. His pants baggy and scratched; his face bruised. "He's got no collar, no tags. He's a stray and he found me."

I think TaShon is a stray. Like me, he doesn't have friends. I read books, do homework. TaShon just walks the neighborhood in his own world. Or sits on his porch staring out. Once I saw him trying to make an ant colony, filling a mason jar with dirt. I asked him if he needed help, but he said, "No," turning his back to me. So, in the neighborhood, I pretty much leave him alone.

"Please, Lanesha. Help me. I know he's not a German shepherd. I just always wanted one."

I look at TaShon. Hard. Really see him. His eyes are brown just like the dog's. He's nice looking. Kind, I think. He has a kind face. He's tiny, though, smaller than most girls.

Patting the dog, he seems happy.

Seeing TaShon's feelings on his face, I see him.

"Please."

"All right. But Mama Ya-Ya might say we should call the dogcatcher."

"No, she won't."

"How you know?"

"I just do." He is one happy boy and I smile. Then, I whistle and call, "Come, Spot," and the dog does, trailing beside me, his stump of a tail high. I have seen much prettier dogs. But Spot doesn't seem to mind being ugly.

❧

"Lookee, here," says Mama Ya-Ya as we walk through the door. "Is that Spot?"

I am *exasperated*. I learned that word from my dictionary. *Exasperated* as in *annoyed*.

Spot lies down at Mama Ya-Ya's feet like he belongs there.

I am *exasperated,* but not surprised. Mama Ya-Ya knows everything. She has the *sight,* too.

She gives both me and Spot a bowl of Hoppin' John.

I look around the warm kitchen as we eat. The gas stove. The dinette set. Mason jars filled with roots and herbs on the counter. Mama Ya-Ya is humming a sweet tune. Some song from her African past, from another life. Spot is snoring slightly at her feet.

When we finish, I do the dishes, watching rainbow bubbles float up from the sink.

❧

"You know, there's a storm coming," says Mama Ya-Ya as I slip the last clean dish on the rack, my hands dripping with water. There's been nothing on the radio or the TV news. Nothing in the papers. But Mama Ya-Ya knows. "By the end of the week."

I shrug. We've had storms before.

"TaShon's coming, too," she says.

I'm always still surprised how Mama Ya-Ya can see people coming before they even get here. Sometimes I think she has more powers than any superhero.

There is a *rat-a-tat-tat* on the screen door. "Lanesha, it's me. TaShon."

Spot gets up wagging his whole body. I look up, drying my hands.

"Y'all clean that dog before bed," says Mama Ya-Ya.

"C'mon," I say to TaShon, opening the door, then moving down the steps, around the side of the house.

TaShon pats Spot. "I always wanted a dog."

I say nothing. Just grab the hose and spray Spot and TaShon both. One shouts, the other howls; both are happy.

It is hot and the water is cold. I toss TaShon a bar of soap and he is scrubbing Spot. I think they both are getting cleaner than they've ever been. Spot licks TaShon's face and TaShon grins. Neighbors pass by.

Mrs. Watson cries, "That is one fine dog. Just a pup."

Mr. Lincoln who has a fake left foot (he says his flesh foot is buried in Vietnam) shouts, "Wash him once. Then, twice. Three times clean. Fleas don't like soap."

Mr. D, Mama Ya-Ya's friend, a retired cop, hoots, "Who's your new friend, Lanesha?"

I look around to see who he's talking about. It's TaShon. TaShon shakes himself, and when he does it, Spot shakes himself, too, spraying water like streamers. TaShon does it again; so does Spot.

"A trick, already?!" exclaims Mr. D. "You've got a smart friend, Lanesha." Mr. D waddles away, his belly wiggling like jelly over his belt. I don't tell him TaShon is our neighbor from across the street.

"Whoop, whoop, whoop," I scream, holding the hose high then low. Spot barks. Soon, him and TaShon are jumping up and down trying to escape the water snake. High, then low. Spot tries to bite the water. TaShon, one eye still closed, just laughs and laughs. I spray his sneakers and Spot's toes.

I wave at Rudy and Rodriguez. They live in the blue shotgun house down the block.

Rudy calls, "Lanesha, spray some here, too." I do and the two grown men laugh like TaShon, jumping back, yet jumping forward enough to make sure their shirts and hair get wet. "Feels good," says Rodriguez. "Our neighborhood rain machine." He tosses a silver dollar to TaShon. "Buy the dog a bone."

TaShon, his arms spread wide, twirls like an airplane. Spot barks and chases his tail. I lift the hose high; water falls like a soft summer shower.

There is sweetness to this day.

I thought this day was going to be ordinary. But it was full of surprises: Andrew, TaShon and Spot, and Miss Johnson saying I could be an engineer.

I look up and down the street. Most folks are outside. None of the houses have air-conditioning. The houses are painted in pastel colors — pink, yellow, blue, and green. A few are white. Only our house is peach. Pastel colors are supposed to be cool, but all of us are sweating just the same.

I hear Mama Ya-Ya's TV news floating yackety-yak out the window: *"A tropical storm is kicking up high waves in the Bahamas. Satellites show the counterclockwise rotation of a developing hurricane. Winds, thirty-eight miles per hour..."*

I hear someone blowing a saxophone. I hear some boys hollering for pickup basketball; others are rapping on the street corner. Pretending they are on TV.

Girls are playing jacks and double Dutch. The older ones are sitting on porches, gossiping, braiding each other's hair, and looking at old copies of *Essence* magazine.

Grown-ups are arriving home from work. They seem like kids again, grinning silly. Their wrinkly faces go all smooth once they park their cars or step down from the city bus. Men take off their jackets like they're slipping off backpacks, and women swing their purses like empty lunch boxes. Retired folks walk through the neighborhood trying to be helpful. They scold kids to walk, not run, across the street.

I spray TaShon's big feet. Spot barks.

I'm happy. I think this neighborhood is my family. Right here. Now.

Who needs a dumb Uptown family?

Wednesday

I wake, stretch. Sun is shining into my room, making my blue walls glow. Spot stretches, too. He slept with me all night. Warm and soft.

I fall back on the pillow and Spot lays his head on me. He licks my face and I say, "Time for school."

Dressed, I pass Mama Ya-Ya's bedroom. It's empty except for my mother's ghost. Lying on the bed, as still as an alligator, sunning.

I ignore her. I've seen her so many times. But Spot

stops. Ears perked, tail and even the hair down his spine up.

"You see her?" I say.

Spot doesn't move.

"It's my mother from long ago. She doesn't mean harm. Most of the time, she sleeps like now. Or just sits and stares."

Spot turns his head and looks at me like he understands everything I say.

"I guess she misses us. Or else she's waiting for something. I don't know what. It's been twelve years."

Spot licks my hand.

I swallow. "I can't touch her. Or talk to her either. Not really. I can talk, but she won't answer back. I don't know why."

Sniffing, Spot lifts his head high into the air. I think: Juliet should've had a dog. She might've been less sad if she'd had a dog.

Spot turns and prances down the stairs.

❧

"Weatherman says a big storm is coming. Might be a hurricane. What I tell you?" Mama Ya-Ya clicks off the fire beneath a pot. "I knew it. Just knew it. I saw the birds leaving their trees. Saw how the water was slow to boil.

"Don't stay after school, Lanesha. I need you to pick up supplies. Milk. Bread. Rice. Beans. Bottled water."

"You think this is going to be another Betsy?" Before I was born, Hurricane Betsy tore up New Orleans. I saw old clips on the news. Mean Betsy. Some of the folks didn't have clean water. Or any food. Mama Ya-Ya wants us to be prepared.

Spot sits, begging at Mama Ya-Ya's skirt. He's already had breakfast. Mama Ya-Ya gives him a piece of toast.

I giggle.

Mama Ya-Ya puts a plate before me. The over-easy egg is bright yellow and white. I puncture the egg and watch the yellow river swirl on my plate. I take hot sauce and sprinkle the runny yolk red.

Instead of cleaning dishes, Mama Ya-Ya sits at the

table with me. Her hair isn't neat. It's matted to her head like she's just gotten out of bed. Mama Ya-Ya never comes to the table without her hair combed! She's also left her teeth in their glass. Her cheeks look hollow.

She sucks air through her gums. It's a brief whistle. Spot comes and lays his head in her lap. She pats Spot's fuzzy head, but she doesn't look at him.

I sit up straight and pay attention.

"I had a dream. Don't know yet what it means."

I'm not worried. Mama Ya-Ya often has dreams. Just as she knows about things before they happen, her dreams can tell her things, too. Sometimes she dreams I'm going to have a pop quiz in school. Vocabulary. Math. So, I'll study extra during breakfast. Orange juice, bacon, and eggs are the perfect study food. If I'm lucky, Mama Ya-Ya will make grits or hash browns, too.

Most times, Mama Ya-Ya's dreams are about who's sick, who's delivering a baby, who got laid off from a job. She dreamed Mr. Bailey was going to break his leg. She told him he was too old to be spreading tar on his roof. But Mr. Bailey waved his hand, saying,

"Seventy plus seven is a lucky number." He slipped off the ladder just the same. For an entire month, he scowled at me, stomped his crutches, whenever I brought him Mama Ya-Ya's fresh-baked pralines.

Usually, breakfast is my favorite time of day. Me and Mama Ya-Ya talk about school ("I want to sail all the blue on the globe," I'll say), whether I need new shoes ("You're growing so big," she'll say), what I want for dinner ("Pork chops," I'll say), and my weekend chores ("Clean the bathroom," she'll say). We talk regular, everyday stuff.

But today, Mama Ya-Ya sits across from me, her brows wrinkling like cornrows. I'm surprised 'cause Mama Ya-Ya usually cleans while I eat. She can't stand dirty pans or a greasy stove.

She is talking to me serious.

"In my dream, Lanesha, storm clouds come; wind comes; rain smacks down; the water clears. Sun comes out. Folks go about their business. Everyone is happy. But then, everything goes black. Like someone pulling a curtain. Or a shroud being pulled over the dead. Or God turning out the lights." She smacks her hand on the counter. And stares at the ceiling like some truth is up there.

I stare, too, but all I see is our kitchen lamp with dead bugs in its glass basin.

I start to feel a wee bit of fear. Usually, Mama Ya-Ya understands her dreams. I am scared not by her dream itself, but because she doesn't seem to know what it means.

Mama Ya-Ya gets up, and picks up the pot of scalded milk from the stove's back burner. "I think the storm might be bad," she says, certain. "But not as bad as Betsy."

She pours me café au lait — mixing the milk from the pot with coffee in my cup. Since I was five, I've been drinking café au lait. It always makes me feel grown-up. Now that I'm older, I realize Mama Ya-Ya doesn't use much coffee. Still, I pretend I'm drinking exactly what Mama Ya-Ya drinks, and not just 99 percent hot milk.

"Momma is upstairs," I say.

"I know. What's she doing?"

"Just sleeping. Though I don't know why a ghost

needs to sleep. She could be sailing the seas. Or flying to Africa."

I don't know why I'm talking about my mother. I used to talk about her a lot when I was little. I wanted to know everything about her, but I discovered there wasn't too much to know.

Mama Ya-Ya pats my head, just like she patted Spot. Pat-pat. I don't mind.

Mama Ya-Ya's eyes are still crinkled with worry. She picks up my plate. The egg and hot sauce has made it glow like yellow, orange, and red finger paint. "Hurry, you'll be late for school," she says.

I grab my notebook of assignment sheets. Even though our schoolbooks are tattered and old, we aren't allowed to bring them home. Spot scurries up. I say, "Stay. Mama Ya-Ya needs company."

"Not with ghosts in the house. Got all the company I need."

"Spot isn't allowed in school. 'Sides, he sees ghosts, too."

"He does?"

Mama Ya-Ya and her cane move closer to Spot. She

is bending, peering down at him. Her Coke-bottle-covered eyes looking into his baby browns. I can tell she's smiling inside. Spot will give her someone to talk to. Mama Ya-Ya, I think, will be chattering away before I'm down the porch steps.

I open the screen door. The sun is ever so bright. I can smell the trees, flowers, and bacon. Everybody in my neighborhood loves bacon. Probably a dozen families are frying it right now.

I turn back and say, "Do you ever think my mother's ever going to stop being here?"

"She'll stop when she finds her purpose. Go on now. You'll be late." Then, "You want some bacon?" she says to Spot.

I smile. Mama Ya-Ya and Spot are going to have a good day.

❧

My day is fine. I even like PE. I run track and win. Ginia pronounced like *Virginia*, without the *Vir*, comes in a close second. Ginia has the biggest smile, an itty-bitty nose, and beautiful cornrows with crystal, rainbow beads. Ginia is popular and cute. Not like me. Every PE class, she's been nice to me. Not stuck-up. I wish she were in one of my other classes. Except for PE, I only see her in the halls with the cheerleading girls who like to stroll after school on the Riverwalk, trying to look cute.

Last week, Ginia even asked me to go try on clothes at the mall. No one has money to buy, but that doesn't change anything. Hours can be spent trying on clothes. Drinking a Big Gulp at the mall.

Still.

I didn't say yes. I think Ginia feels sorry for me. I don't need anyone's sorry. 'Sides, even if she was sincere, her friends wouldn't be. Sooner or later someone will bring up my weird eyes. Or say, "You see dead people." Or false-pity me not having parents, calling me an "orphan girl" or worse. More worse, they'd call Mama Ya-Ya a "witch." Then, I'd have to fight. I like Ginia too much to ruin her good time.

Still. She keeps asking. I think it's because she didn't go to my elementary school. She doesn't know that I've always been on my own — except for Mama Ya-Ya and the neighbors who watched me grow for a long time.

"Lanesha, after school want to hear my CDs? I got some new ones." Ginia is smiling, her hands on her knees, still panting from running.

"I can't."

"You always say that."

I'm tempted. "Mama Ya-Ya wants me to go to the store."

"I'll go with you."

My eyes widen. But I only say, "Okay."

All through math, I'm distracted. I don't think Ginia means what she says; still, I hope. Wonder if she'll wait for me after school?

At lunch, I eat my tuna sandwich and apple juice at my table. I call it "my table," 'cause no one will sit with me. But, unlike TaShon, I don't try to be invisible. I sit right in the middle of the cafeteria. I'm not ashamed of me. In class, folks don't like to sit near me, either.

In my old school, teachers used to make them. Then, there'd be hollering, "I don't wanna. I don't wanna." I guess when teachers figured out sitting by myself didn't bother me, they let it go. It does bother me that kids don't sit beside me. I just don't let it show. During lunch, I read; during class, I stare at the teacher and blackboard. I blot out all the kids being rude! I sometimes imagine that they're just ghosts, too.

But today I am itching with thoughts of Ginia.

Twice, Miss Johnson asks what's wrong with me. I can't answer her. Part of me feels embarrassed, and I'm not sure why.

But I watch the clock, anyhow; its hands measure time, superslow. I tell myself I know better than to want something so bad. If my Uptown family has taught me anything, it's taught me that. If I thought it would add up to anything, I wouldn't hang out with Ginia after school. Why worry that once she found out about me, she might diss me like my Uptown relatives?

Click. Finally, the clock's big hand points twelve. Its little hand points three. The school bell rings.

I steel my heart. I won't get hurt.

I didn't think buying milk, bread, and water could be so much fun. Mr. Ng owns the corner store and him and Ginia talk about his daughter, Mengying, in Vietnam.

"We're pen pals," says Ginia. "When Mr. Ng has enough money, he'll send for Mengying. When we're older, she's going to show me Vietnam. The land of a thousand temples."

"Put it on Mama Ya-Ya's account," I say, pointing at the bread, milk, and water on the counter.

"Sure thing," says Mr. Ng. He knows neighborhood Social Security, disability, and welfare checks come in first of the month. Mama Ya-Ya always pays. She stretches her Social Security to include me. It is Wednesday, the twenty-fourth. On the first of the month, we'll feel rich (have fresh shrimp and hot andouille sausage); on the second, we'll be poor again.

"Is Mama Ya-Ya planning on a hurricane?" asks

Mr. Ng. "Weatherman says big hurricane coming to Florida."

"She says a storm's coming. Told me we had to prepare."

"Mama Ya-Ya's ghosts say so? Prepare? Storm's coming to New Orleans? Or hurricane? Her ghosts say which?"

Mr. Ng understands ghosts. He told Mama Ya-Ya that Vietnam was filled with them. From time to time, the two of them talk about ointments and roots. Mr. Ng confides his worries about his ancestors. He hopes his cousins in Vietnam are caring for his parents' graves. Mama Ya-Ya says, "I understand." Then, Mama Ya-Ya hugs him. Mr. Ng bows. Their conversation is always the same.

"Not ghosts this time, Mr. Ng," I answer, shy to be talking about ghosts in front of Ginia. "She dreamed it," I say, wincing that these words are no better. Ginia will leave me soon enough. Just wait. "Ghosts, dreams," she'll say, disgusted, thinking I'm too crazy to bother with.

I grab the bags and go.

Outside, it's cloudy, shrill with wind blowing through the cypress trees. The sun seems to have disappeared.

"My grandmother sees things, too," says Ginia. "We just don't talk about it."

I smile. Ginia smiles back. She slips her hand over mine and grabs the bag with milk and water.

The humidity is high. It is still New Orleans hot. Mosquitoes are eating my neck.

❧

Up ahead, there's a crowd on Mr. Palmer's porch. He's an amputee. Both his legs are gone because of diabetes. Every day his wife rolls his wheelchair onto the porch with a TV stand and a small color TV. His pug, Beanie, curls up beneath where his feet ought to be. Both spend their days on the porch until Mrs. Palmer comes home from making beds at the Hilton. If it rains, Mrs. Palmer knows neighbors will take Mr. Palmer inside. She leaves him a pitcher of beer and a paper sack filled with sandwiches for lunch. A bone for Beanie. Neighbors drifting by will sometimes leave pecans or an apple. Everybody knows not to leave sweets.

"Let's go see," says Ginia.

We walk up onto the porch, saying, "Hey, Mr. Palmer." He nods.

Six or seven people are standing around the small TV. No one says much. I recognize Rudy, Mrs. Watson, and some kids from the school. Max is there — but he doesn't pay me any mind. Everyone stares at the TV.

I press in, too, watching the weatherman with a big head of blond hair. His stick is pointing at lines and names on the screen. There are blue, green, brown colors; all good colors; blue means happiness; green, nature; brown, earth. The Atlantic Ocean is blue. Florida sticks out like a green and brown thumb. But the weatherman keeps scratching at his collar like he can't get enough air. He makes me nervous. There's a white circle cloud, too, twisting slowly on the small screen. White is sacred, pure. In the cloud's center, it's red. The red glows, contracting, then growing bigger than before. It has already passed over islands. Now it is rushing towards southern Florida.

Mama Ya-Ya says red can mean love or energy. Or blood, danger.

I realize the TV sound isn't on, but none of us needs to hear the man speak. We can all see. On the bottom of the screen, it says, "Hurricane Katrina, Category One."

❦

Ginia and I walk to my porch. I don't want to think about the colors on TV. I want to think about having more fun with Ginia. But the TV pictures have already changed the neighborhood. Grown-ups, their hands shading their eyes, are looking at the sky, worried. Some folks are unloading gallons of water from their cars; others, zombielike, instead of waving or saying hello when we pass by, keep staring at baby TVs or listening to boom box radios.

Ginia sets the milk and water down, and turns to go.

NINTH WARD

Jewell Parker Rhodes

NINTH WARD

Jewell Parker Rhodes

PRAISE FOR *NINTH WARD*

"Jewell's vivid writing brings the setting to life, in a story that is both timely and unforgettable." —Patricia Reilly Giff

"Another gem by Jewell Parker Rhodes." —Nikki Giovanni

Rejected by her peers because of her ability to see spirits, Lanesha longs for a connection. The one true light in her life is her fiercely loving caretaker, Mama Ya-Ya. When Hurricane Katrina lands and tragedy strikes, Lanesha is forced to come into her own in order to survive the storm.

A gorgeously written coming-of-age novel set in New Orleans during Hurricane Katrina.

LB

LITTLE, BROWN AND COMPANY
BOOKS FOR YOUNG READERS

www.ninthwardbook.com

www.lbschoolandlibrary.com

"Don't you want to come inside?"

"I do, but—"

"Is that your new friend?" Mama Ya-Ya hollers from inside the house. "Is it Ginger? Virginia? Ginia?"

Ginia's eyes open wide.

"Mama Ya-Ya already knows about you. Like I told you, she sees without seeing." Through the screen door, I holler back at Mama Ya-Ya, "It's just a girl from school."

"No, I'm not. I mean, I am, but I'm not—"

Now, it's my turn to be bug-eyed.

"I'll be needed at home, Lanesha. What with the weather and all."

"Okay," I say. Then, feeling bold, I say, "See you tomorrow?" (Though I guess if I felt really bold, I wouldn't have let my voice rise with a question.) I cross my fingers behind my back.

Ginia leaps down onto the sidewalk. Her tennis shoes land, making a big *smack*. I think I was wrong about something. Ginia doesn't look cute at all. She looks strong, like she does when she's racing me. How'd I miss that?

"You're lucky, Lanesha." Ginia, her voice bright, hollers over her shoulder, "Tell Mama Ya-Ya she got my name right. I hope I get to meet her next time."

No one has ever said "lucky" about me before. Butterflies flutter in my chest.

"Bye," I say. But I'm not sure Ginia hears me. She races down my street towards her house, at least five blocks over. Her tennis shoes kick up dust.

That night, after dinner, I draw bridges. Big ones. Small ones. One as towering as the Golden Gate Bridge. The rug tickles my stomach. The pictures, spread all over the floor, make me happy. I grab my pocket dictionary and look up *suspension*. SUSPEN-SION BRIDGE: A BRIDGE HAVING THE ROADWAY SUSPENDED FROM CABLES, ANCHORED AT EITHER END, AND SUPPORTED AT INTERVALS BY TOWERS.

Mama Ya-Ya stands in front of the TV, trying to unravel what the picture means. I'm watching, too. The weatherman's colors are one big puzzle. There is more blue, showing the Atlantic and the Gulf of Mexico. The white cloud with the red heart is moving. It looks both pretty and scary. I stop drawing, looking for a sign about what the TV picture means. The weatherman is chattering, pointing at the colors with his stick.

I realize he is talking math — "if, then" problems like I study in school.

"*If the wind blows south, then, the hurricane might miss the entire Gulf region.*

"*If the hurricane loosens, becomes diffuse, then, there might be only a tropical storm for Florida, Mississippi, and Louisiana.*

"*If Katrina keeps gathering strength, then, depending where she lands, the damage could be great.*"

The weatherman doesn't have the certainty of my math problems. There doesn't seem to be one right answer. The answer could be *a*, *b*, or *c*.

Mama Ya-Ya keeps standing, leaning on her cane, staring at the TV. I realize she's looking for meaning, too.

I go to the window and stick my head out. The sky is velvet black and the moon is bright white. The air seems thick, moist, and still. I can't imagine that elsewhere there is a hurricane. Racing rain and wind. I can't see it. But that doesn't mean it doesn't exist.

People can't see spirits so they don't believe they exist, but I know they do.

My stomach starts to ache. I hear hammering. Across the street, someone is nailing planks across their front windows.

Mama Ya-Ya is still watching the TV. Tonight, it seems like the weatherman is the star.

I settle back down on the floor where my pretty bridges are scattered, enjoying how warm and cozy our living room is.

I grab the *Encyclopedia Britannica*. Volume B.

Mama Ya-Ya paid $3 a week for three years until she'd paid for the entire encyclopedia set. It was my best present ever. The books have their own special shelf. The only other book on the shelf is Mama Ya-Ya's Bible. She reads it over and over again, and tells me its stories. I like the story of David beating the giant, Goliath. Of baby Moses being rescued from the water.

Atop the bookshelf is a picture of Mama Ya-Ya holding my hand when I was two. I look different now. Mama Ya-Ya looks the same, wise and beautiful.

I sit on the floor, opening the huge book. The cover is getting worn, but the insides are just fine. Like Mama Ya-Ya, the words and pictures keep teaching me.

As it gets darker and darker outside, I ignore the TV and read about bridges, famous builders, and the engineers who imagined the mathematical symbols and signs that people can't see. I wonder how something that starts off so invisible turns into metal, bolts, and wires, connecting point A to point B.

Thursday

August 25.

Mama Ya-Ya has both the radio and TV on. She's been up since dawn. Me and Spot are both worried about her. She keeps walking between the two — listening to radio sounds, watching the local news. She mutters, "The storm ain't the problem. The storm ain't the problem." She still has not used the word *hurricane.*

I watch the TV for a minute. "Katrina is a Category Two hurricane," says the weatherman, "quickly becoming a Category Three." What does Category Two or Three mean? The white spirals of storm have gotten bigger on the TV map. The storm is spinning over the Gulf, heading towards Mississippi and Louisiana. I see a dot on the map and the words NEW ORLEANS. I realize that the colors are not so important after all; it's the dot and the growing size and faster spin of the clouds.

The TV shows pictures from Florida: a man unable to stand because of wind, cars abandoned, trees lying on the ground. The weatherman says: "In Florida, several are reported missing and the damages are in the millions. While Katrina was just a Category One, she was slow moving, causing greater than normal damage. Now she's two, on her way to becoming three times more powerful. When she lands again, the destruction will be unfathomable."

Unfathomable. I need to look it up. I can guess what it means, but I want to know exactly.

Mama Ya-Ya is touching the TV screen as if her palm can stop the storm.

Every year, we have hurricane season. Hurricanes hit Florida. Texas. Mississippi. I've seen storm troubles in New Orleans, too — flooding, a fallen tree, a roof blown off. Every year, folks say, "Hurricane season is going to be bad." But it never is. I think Katrina will die before she lands. She's already messed up Florida. Shown how bad she is. What else could she want?

Mama Ya-Ya taught me hurricanes are Mother Nature's fits. "We don't expect people to be quiet all the time," she likes to say. "Why nature?" Two sides to everything, everyone. Good and bad. Quiet and loud. Calm, stormy.

Still. *Unfathomable.* The word bothers me. So does Mama Ya-Ya this morning. I know she's really worried because she hasn't fixed me breakfast or café au lait. She is swaying side to side like a windblown tree. The house doesn't smell of food. And Mama Ya-Ya doesn't smell sharply sweet, coolly warm.

She's forgotten her Vicks Rub and Evening in Paris perfume.

"I'm off to school."

"Sure, baby," Mama Ya-Ya answers.

I stoop and rub Spot's ears. He is lying on the rug, his tongue hanging out. "Take care of her."

Spot licks my ear.

I don't say "Bye," 'cause I don't think Mama Ya-Ya will hear me.

From the living room, I walk across the hall, ignoring the front door, and walk through the kitchen. I'm used to leaving through the back door.

"Hey, Lanesha." The shadow and light through the screen make squares on TaShon's face. "I came over to see Spot."

Spot, who hears everything, races to the screen door.

"TaShon, you gonna be late for school."

"Ain't no school."

"You lie."

"No, I don't," says TaShon, opening the door and leaning down to rub his nose on Spot's fur. "You're my good dog."

I wince. TaShon is silly. I'm feeling irritated. *Exasperated.* "You should take your good dog home."

I don't like to see Spot loving him with the same licks he gives me. And TaShon, who didn't say "boo" to me for years, is acting like I invited him in to stay.

"Go on, now. Both of you."

TaShon sits back on his heels, biting his bottom lip. Even Spot's tail droops. "For real, Lanesha? You know my momma won't let me keep him. She'll say, 'We can't afford another mouth to feed.' She'll call animal control. Have him jailed. Please, Lanesha. You've got to keep him."

"I'm just foolin'," I say, starting to feel guilty. TaShon smiles like it's Christmas. He falls backward, rumpling Spot. I can't help but smile, too.

I step onto the back porch. The sun is warm and the sky is cloudless.

"There's got to be school," I say. It's hard enough that there's a Saturday and Sunday. I'm less lonely at school with my teachers and books.

"There's not."

"I'll see for myself."

"The mayor says folks ought to think about leaving New Orleans. People are packing up."

"You going?"

TaShon shrugs. "I don't know." Then, he pretend growls and soon, him and Spot, like big babies, are leaping off the porch and rolling in the crabgrass.

I walk out the door.

TaShon was right. School's been canceled and the empty hallways are filling with ghosts. Usually they stay away when us kids are loud, playing in the hallways. But the hurricane warning has emptied people out and ghosts, from when our school used to be a convent, are filling the halls. Mainly nuns. Sisters of Charity. A priest or two.

The ghost nuns in their black robes look like they're gliding on ice. One of them waves at me. Sister Margaret. She likes school, too. Especially English when we're discussing stories, instead of diagramming sentences.

The ghosts look distracted by the silence, the empty halls. Mostly, they keep their heads bowed low.

I walk the halls, looking for Miss Johnson. She is my favorite teacher by far.

❧

Miss Johnson is packing a box. The classroom is empty, and she's packing her pictures of her momma and poppa and sisters and nieces. She's packing the cardboard signs she bought with her own money: EVERYTHING IS MATH; WITH NUMBERS, YOU CAN DO ANYTHING; DISCOVER X, THE GREAT UNKNOWN.

"You leaving?" I say, stupid, 'cause I already know the answer.

"Soon as I'm packed up here, I'm getting on the road. My folks were in Betsy. I don't mess with hurricanes."

I don't know what comes over me because I start to cry. Miss Johnson pretends not to see.

I haven't cried in a long time. I'm angry at myself. Can't think why I'm crying. Except too much is happening. Both good and bad. I don't like to see Mama Ya-Ya worried. The thought of Ginia, TaShon, and Spot makes me happy. But it's all too fast. What if Ginia and TaShon decide not to like me? What if the storm does come? Should Mama Ya-Ya and I leave, too? I don't have time to puzzle it out. Fit these tiny new pieces together to see what picture it might make.

"I'll be back," Miss Johnson says. "Are you all right, Lanesha?"

"What?" I say, my voice cracking a little.

"Leaving probably means nothing much is going to happen. We'll have school on Monday. Just think of this as a holiday. Like a surprise long weekend."

"I don't want a holiday."

"Well, I do. I'm tired. School just started and I could use a rest. I'm going to visit my folks in Baton Rouge." She comes over to me. "Surely you don't mind me getting rest?"

"No, ma'am," I say, though I know she's only twenty-two. I wipe my cheeks.

"Is your family leaving?"

I tilt my head, wondering what family she means. Uptown or Mama Ya-Ya?

"You should leave," she says, looking at me directly. "Just in case."

Miss Johnson, I realize, is really not that much older than me. Studying her face, I can see I could one day be her. Educated. A schoolteacher.

I blurt, "I could be you."

"No, you can't," she says, making me hurt inside. "You're you. Lanesha. You're much smarter than me. Better with numbers than me at your age. What about being an engineer?"

I smile. "And I'll build bridges like the Golden Gate Bridge. The Bridge of Sighs in Venice. The London Tower Bridge."

"I see you've been studying."

"Yes, ma'am. The encyclopedia has dozens of pictures of bridges and waterways. New Orleans has the Crescent City Bridge and the Huey P. Long Bridge," I say, remembering all those steel puzzles reaching towards the sky.

"Or Lanesha's Bridge? You could build a bridge and name it after you."

This is why I like this new school. Teachers fill my head with pictures and thoughts about what *I* can do. "I'll name it after you. Evelyn," I say. "Evelyn's Bridge."

Miss Johnson smiles. "Got to go, Lanesha. You be safe."

I start to walk away but turn back. "Miss Johnson, can you give me a problem to work on?"

Miss Johnson smiles; she understands. A problem will keep my mind off the hurricane.

She looks at me. Then, she turns and unlocks her desk and pulls out a book. "Take this. It's the teacher's edition."

"Really? You think I'm ready?"

"Most def'," says Miss Johnson, trying to sound cool. I laugh.

It is a nice blue copy of pre-algebra. Not tattered and marked like the student workbooks. The book smells new, fresh with ink. This is a seventh-grade book.

"I know you won't cheat. There are tons of problems."

"And I can check my answers?"

"Yes. Just start at the beginning. Read careful. Take it slow."

I'm so happy, stroking the slick pages, seeing hundreds of squiggly marks.

"See you on Monday, Lanesha."

"See you on Monday, Miss Johnson." I look down at the book. Then, back at her. "Thank you."

"Who knows," she says, turning back to her boxes, "if the storm gets worse, you may even finish the whole book."

"*If the storm gets worse...If the storm gets worse...*" These words echo in my head as I walk out the door.

Friday

Mama Ya-Ya will not go to bed.

And now, there are ghosts in the living room. I'm used to seeing a random one every now and again, but tonight it feels crowded. A thin man dressed like a Confederate soldier. A little girl with braids and pink pajamas with padded feet. I wonder if they lived here. In Mama Ya-Ya's house? Or in the neighborhood? Maybe the soldier just marched by and decided to stay. New Orleans has all kinds of people who arrived and never left.

Me and the ghosts keep watching the TV.

TaShon has taken Spot for a walk. Mama Ya-Ya is outside using her senses: sniffing for sea salt, feeling hot wind, listening for the roar of water. I don't know if she can taste a hurricane. What would it taste like? Like cold, fishy, salty cotton candy?

The TV says the governor has asked the president to declare a state of emergency. The National Guard has been called up. Now the breathless weatherman is saying the hurricane will hit Mississippi and Louisiana. Both.

I'm feeling **ANXIOUS**: FULL OF ANXIETY. GREATLY CONCERNED, ESPECIALLY ABOUT SOMETHING IN THE FUTURE OR UNKNOWN.

I'm feeling more anxious because I looked up *unfathomable* in my pocket dictionary. **UNFATHOMABLE**: BEYOND UNDERSTANDING, IMPOSSIBLE TO MEASURE.

In math, I learned everything can be measured. Air, water, wind. Volume. Velocity. Depth.

So why not a hurricane? There, I've said it.

Hurricane Katrina. Two words. Three syllables each.

The TV shows folks partying in the French Quarter.

Dancing, laughing. Music playing. Everybody's having a good time. A reporter in a navy blue dress, with cool earrings dangling from her ears, asks a man and woman: "What do you think of the hurricane?" The man answers, holding up a glass that looks like he has a strawberry slush. He swallows and says, "The weather's just fine." Then, him and the woman start twirling around.

Another reporter shows a family across town. A father and son, both red haired, are locking white shutters over their windows. Then, the father speaks in a gruff voice into the microphone: "We're staying right here. I've survived many hurricane seasons. Like the Boy Scouts say, 'Be prepared.' See." He points inside his garage. "I've got gallons of water. Canned goods. Extra fuel. Candles. Matches. A flashlight. Behind back, I have a generator." The man smiles, proud of himself. Then, he yells, "Sean, come over here. Say hi."

Sean is skinnier than his dad. He looks like he's in high school. He looks right into the camera and waves and I think he is waving at me.

I get up and go outside. Usually, the street is quiet after 9:00 p.m. But I can tell some of the neighbors are loading up cars with suitcases. Others are unloading wood, two-by-fours. Then, I remember from civics class that storm winds will break glass. Window shutters, if you can afford them, are easiest and best. But planks of wood across windows can be just as good. Even if you leave your house, I remember reading, it's best to board it up.

Mama Ya-Ya is sitting on the porch step. I plop down beside her.

"Mama Ya-Ya, are you okay?"

"I've been looking for butterflies."

I look around. "Butterflies don't fly at night," I say, feeling sure. "Do they?"

Mama Ya-Ya doesn't answer. She's so beautiful, I think. But I can see she's tired. Dark shadows are beneath her eyes.

I'm lucky to have her raising me. After all this time, I sometimes forget she's not my blood relative.

In Ninth Ward, some folks claim grandchildren

when their parents are dead. Or if their parents are missing, like in jail, rehab. The government can give grandparents money for food and health. But Mama Ya-Ya's not a relative. And Mama Ya-Ya never went to court to be my foster mom or legal guardian. She feared a judge would say she's too old; or worse, send me to live with relatives who didn't want me.

Even though we sometimes have to "stretch a dollar," I've never been hungry. Never been cold. Or without a bed. For special occasions, I get math workbooks with stickers from the drugstore. Sometimes, a book from the library's used book sale or new pencils with fresh erasers. Or a red pocket dictionary. Or a set of sparkly birthday pens.

"Love is as love does," Mama Ya-Ya says. And she has loved me.

"Mama Ya-Ya," I say, "I'm going to go to Mr. Ng's store. I think I should get more water. Canned foods. Is that okay? We can put it on account?"

Mama Ya-Ya looks at me. Her eyes are so kind. "Sure, baby. Sure."

"I'll hurry back." Up to now, Mama Ya-Ya has always insisted I stay inside the house after 8:00 p.m., finishing my homework, getting ready for bed.

I jump from the steps and the *smack* sound of my tennis shoes makes me think of Ginia. I hope she's okay. I hope we get to hang out together soon.

I run down the street. It's so busy for so late at night. But no one says hi. All the grown-ups seem busy like bees.

I get to Ng Grocery and there is no sign of Mr. Ng. There is a CLOSED sign in the window, even though a sign on the door says, OPEN 6 A.M. TO 11 P.M. It can't be later than 10:00 p.m.

I peer into the store. The lights are still on, but the shelves are bare. No cornflakes, no rice, no water, or milk. Nothing. Not a single can of food. Have Mr. Ng and his family left New Orleans?

I start home but I don't run. I walk. Everything is topsy-turvy like in *Alice in Wonderland*. Except it's a white cloud's fault, not a rabbit hole's.

A white cloud spinning across the TV has turned my neighborhood upside down, inside out.

Saturday

In the morning, when I wake, Mama Ya-Ya's standing over my bed. She scares me because I think she's one of my ghosts. But Spot doesn't bark, so I calm down and see it is Mama Ya-Ya with her Coke-bottle glasses on the top of her head.

I don't know how long she's been standing there, watching me sleep.

"Are you okay, Mama Ya-Ya?"

"I'm fine," she says. "You know how much I love you?"

"Yes. I do." Though, most often, Mama Ya-Ya never says the word *love*. She just shows me. Each and every day. When she buys me a scented soap from Walgreens. Or fixes me grits with butter and sugar. When she asks, "Did you finish your homework?" Or "Play cards with me?"

"I was glad," Mama Ya-Ya says, her voice scratchy, "when your momma wanted me to help birth you. I buried your caul in the backyard, but not before I said prayers, laid down roots with it. And not before I took a drop of its blood and made a tea for your momma to get strong."

Mama Ya-Ya has never told me this before. I want to ask: Where'd you bury the caul? Is it beneath the magnolia tree? Beneath my bedroom window? In the flower bed?

Instead, I keep quiet and listen hard.

"My tea didn't work because your momma didn't want it to work. Spells, charms, roots can only do so much. All the root workers...all us folks who believe in faiths born in Africa know that.

"I sometimes think your momma chose to leave you with me. She knew I'd love you. Like my own. She knew my loving you would keep me strong."

But, I think, Mama Ya-Ya no longer seems so strong.

She points her finger at me. "Just remember, Lanesha. Don't feed the storm. The storm takes, the storm gives." Then, she is gone. Shuffling, leaning on her cane.

For some reason I want to cry.

I go to the window, poke my head out into the hot, damp air. It seems an ordinary August day.

Don't feed the storm.

But the creature is already feeding on warm Gulf water. Feeding on moist air, sucking it in. Becoming a monster. I get angry. How dare the storm worry Mama Ya-Ya!

I don't know what to do.

I grab the pre-algebra teacher's edition. A pad and a pencil and eraser. In bed, under the covers, I solve the hardest problems.

In the afternoon, the TV announces an EMERGENCY message. I sit on the couch beside Mama Ya-Ya. The reporters in the TV studio and those on location in City Hall are chattering, saying the same thing over and over. "Emergency." "The mayor will speak."

Then, everybody quiets when the mayor comes out. He looks straight into the camera and says everybody should get out. "Now. Leave New Orleans." Flat, just like that. "Leave New Orleans. This is a mandatory evacuation. Mandatory."

Mama Ya-Ya bites her lip, shakes her head, muttering, "How can it be mandatory if I don't have a way to go?"

I feel like screaming. I want to leave. I'm superscared. But if I tell Mama Ya-Ya, I may upset her more.

I can't sit on the sofa anymore.

I get up and go outside. My street is not the same. It's busier, crazier, with more activity than last night.

In front of Mrs. Watson's house, there are three

cars with boxes and suitcases on the roofs. Mrs. Watson's son, Ernie, is yelling, "Ma! Hurry up."

"I don't know what to take," Mrs. Watson wails.

"Don't matter," says Ernie. "We'll be back. Come on, now."

Mrs. Watson, when she sees me, rushes down the steps. "Lanesha, we're going to Baton Rouge. You and Mama Ya-Ya come, too."

"Momma, there ain't no room," shouts Ernie.

Ernie's wife is holding a baby on her hip. Mrs. Watson's other children are with them, too. Four Watson kids and each of the four kids has two kids; one has three.

It'll be one uncomfortable ride in the three cars. Good thing Mr. Watson is a ghost, I think. I see him. Shaking his head, standing behind Mrs. Watson. He's trying to comfort her, but she's too busy worrying about me to feel him.

Most people would *feel* ghosts if they let themselves. But most folks are ignorant on purpose or else too busy, too scared. Real folks ignore any kind of magic.

I say, "Go on, Mrs. Watson. My people are coming for me and Mama Ya-Ya."

"Truly?" Mrs. Watson says, relieved. Ernie wipes his sweaty brow. "I knew your family would one day come to their senses."

"Truly," I say. I start walking. Raise my hand high as a wave. But I don't look back.

No one is coming for Mama Ya-Ya and me. I feel shame. Even if my Uptown relatives don't want me, at least they could rescue Mama Ya-Ya. They owe her for taking care of me all these years, I think.

For the first time, I realize that Mama Ya-Ya is kind of an orphan like me. She and I don't have any other people, except each other.

I wipe tears from my face.

Me and Mama Ya-Ya, we don't need anyone, I think. We're fine.

I pass Rudy and Rodriguez's house. "Mojitos," Rudy shouts, lifting his glass to me.

Rodriguez hits him. "She's too young."

"Y'all leaving?"

"No," says Rudy. "Mojitos are fine for riding out storms. Tropical drink for tropical weather."

I smile, feeling good that they are staying. Comforted that we won't be alone.

Neither Mama Ya-Ya nor I can drive. We don't own a car. If we got to anywhere, we wouldn't have any money. Mama Ya-Ya's Social Security check doesn't come until September 1.

I walk to the end of the block. Aunt Ernestine — she's called that by everyone — is shelling pole beans on her porch. Two kids — Donelle and Faith — are playing jacks behind her. She's got a calico cat that sometimes lives with them — it comes and goes.

Aunt Ernestine is raising her sister's kids — all five of them. Every Sunday, she dresses the children for church. Cleans their faces, and wipes Vaseline on them to keep them from being "ashy." They all walk in a line — nine years old down to five. The baby is carried by Ernestine. I wonder if tomorrow they'll go to church.

I wave.

Aunt Ernestine waves back, smiling. "Trust in the Lord."

I think Aunt Ernestine can't afford to leave either. Or else she's not afraid like Rudy and Rodriguez.

"Yes ma'am," I say; then, I turn and head back down my street.

❧

"TaShon!"

He runs up to me, his face serious. "You'll take care of Spot?"

TaShon's dad is sitting on a sad-looking motorbike, and he's yelling at TaShon to get on.

TaShon grabs my hands. My fingers feel his stumps, where his sixth fingers were trying to grow. "You'll take care of Spot? Promise. Promise. He's my good dog."

"Your only dog," I say.

Then, TaShon hugs me and I'm startled. "You're my best friend."

I hug TaShon back.

His father rolls his eyes, curses.

I whisper: "Where you going?"

"Superdome. The mayor says it'll be open tomorrow morning. My dad wants to get in line."

I can't imagine waiting in line all night for a chance to sleep in the Superdome, where the Saints play football and the cheerleaders jump and scream.

TaShon squeezes me so tight I can barely breathe. We are kin. Both lonely.

I hug some more. With all my might.

He looks at me, clear and hard. Looking at me up close, rather than looking at who knows what far away.

"I'll take care of Spot."

"Swear?"

"TaShon," his father shouts. "We've got to go. Your momma's waiting on us."

"Swear," I say, thinking me and TaShon aren't complete kin. He has a mom and pop looking out for him.

"Lanesha," TaShon says. "Ginia was by earlier looking for you."

"She was?"

"Yeah. She knocked at your door, but no one answered."

My heart is racing.

"She told me to tell you, 'See you soon.'"

"She did?" I'm acting stupid, asking to hear again what TaShon just told me.

"TaShon!"

"Got to go." He races off and gets on the motorbike, wrapping his hands around his father's waist. "TaShon," I shout. "Is Ginia at the Superdome?"

TaShon twists his head, his hand cups his mouth. "Said she was going," he yells over the motorbike roar.

I wave and wave. I think: I will protect Spot with my life. Ginia and I will be friends after the storm.

I watch TaShon and his pop motor down the street.

I think: Look back, TaShon. Look back. I stare and stare at his bobbing head. The motorbike billows smoke. Look back, TaShon. I'm surprised by my feelings.

Two days ago, I just knew TaShon as the short, weird, quiet kid in my neighborhood and class, and now I feel like I've known him forever. Which I have. But it's all different. I know TaShon protects dogs, and he trusts me enough to share Spot, and he, somehow, knew that it mattered to me that Ginia came looking for me.

I see the signs. I couldn't before.

There. TaShon turned his head. Smiling, he's looking back at me. I jump, excited. Then, he and his pop disappear, motoring far, far away.

❧

I stand in the middle of the street. On either side of me, folks are packing cars to leave, hammering wood over windows, or else standing, sitting on the porch, playing music, drinking liquor like it's Mardi Gras.

No one is paying attention to me.

I turn towards home.

I'm feeling happier. A little less scared. TaShon has looked out for me. I will look out for him.

And Spot.

When I see Ginia again, I'll give her a drawing of a bridge. I have a feeling she'll like it.

Still Saturday

It's almost evening and the living room is filled with my bridges. I have been drawing them all afternoon. They make me feel safe, like this is an ordinary weekend day. The setting sun through the window makes them glow, and I imagine walking across the bridges, one by one.

"I don't understand it." Mama Ya-Ya is tapping her cane on the floor. "I've smelled the air, felt the dirt, searched the sky, and listened. All my signs tell me the hurricane is a big one but it should be fine. But I don't *feel* fine. Whenever I lay down, I dream. A big, black shroud. Lanesha, I don't know what it means. I need you to ask your ghosts."

"What?"

"I know you see them."

"But you see them, too."

"I know I do. But I have to work hard to see them. With you, it's a gift. They'll respond to you. You're partly their kind. Feet bridging two worlds. Just try it, baby. I'm worried. Something's coming. Not just a hurricane."

Mama Ya-Ya has never asked for my help with these things before. Her eyes blink big behind her glasses.

Mama Ya-Ya always said I should ignore the ghosts. "They are just like trees, pieces of furniture. Just there. Don't pay them no mind."

She said once I start talking to them, I may never stop. "It's not bad talking to ghosts. Just bad if you want a 'more normal life' in this here world."

I've never understood what that means. *Normal.* If I were normal, I wouldn't be living with Mama Ya-Ya.

I'd be living in a house with a mother and father and with my own dog.

I don't answer Mama Ya-Ya right away. I'm thinking. Even when she pulls me close to her on the couch, her arm wrapped about my shoulders, I'm thinking hard. We watch the TV in silence, our knees touching, and the humidity rising, sucking the air out of the room. The white swirls are nearly eating up the weatherman's map now — and every few minutes, there's some new thing about the storm on its way.

The TV flashes pictures. "The highways are bumper-to-bumper," says a male reporter. "When gas runs out, they just get out and walk. See, that family there. Hitchhiking. Thousands of folks are trying to leave New Orleans." Another picture. "Even though it's a mandatory evacuation, the mayor is allowing those who don't have the money to leave to spend the night in the Superdome." I lean forward, trying to see if I can see TaShon or Ginia in the sea of people on the screen.

Another picture. An old man with gap teeth is on his front lawn, shouting into the microphone:

"Where would I go? This my home. If go to the Super-dome, who's going to protect my house?" Behind him is a crowd of men — mostly young — jumping up and down, trying to get on TV.

I see *chaos*. Another good word. I see Mama Ya-Ya's truly scared. She hasn't combed her hair again, and it's standing on end, every which way. I'm nervous.

I look around to calm myself. Me and Mama Ya-Ya have prepared some. Food. Check. Water. Check. Flashlight. Check. We've even put all the porch fur-niture in the shed. And like always, in case of emer-gency, in case me and Mama Ya-Ya get separated, I know I'm to go to Missionary Baptist Church. But I still feel on edge.

"You want me to get your blood pressure medi-cine?" I ask barely above a whisper.

"I'm fine." She gets up and sits in her rocker, star-ing at the TV screen. "No, I'm not fine." Reaches into her housedress pocket and opens her bottle of pills. "Hand me that water, baby."

I give her the glass and watch as she swallows the

pill and water. Mama Ya-Ya looks older than I've ever seen her.

"My dreams say the city should be fine. Then, the dreams say, 'Not fine.' Doesn't make sense. Either the hurricane is fine or it ain't. Either the city survives or it don't."

I know she wants to say, "Ask your ghosts, Lanesha. Ask them." But she doesn't.

I look around the living room. The good sofa is covered in plastic. On the side table are little black angels. Some are chipped. Some are faded. Mama Ya-Ya has had them since she was a girl. On the wall and on the coffee table are photos of Mama Ya-Ya when she was young, beautiful. In one picture, she is holding hands with Private Charles. He's skinny with a wide smile and black, velvet eyes. He died in World War II. They never married or had children. Afterwards, the girl in the photo stopped being Delores and became Mama Ya-Ya. Midwife. Healer.

"I don't see any ghosts right now," I say. "Maybe they went to the Superdome, too."

"Humph," says Mama Ya-Ya. "What about your momma?"

I blink. Mama Ya-Ya is truly scared. Else she'd never ask me to talk to my mother. She always said starting a conversation with her might bring me a mess of sorrow for what couldn't be, for what was lost.

"Go on, child. I wouldn't ask if it wasn't serious. I'm old and thought I'd seen everything. Understood all that needed understanding. I don't understand this. Dreams that say Orleans still stands after the hurricane. But the streets still flood with sadness.

"I don't know if I should move you from danger. But I can't figure out what the danger is. Maybe you should see if the Watsons left? Maybe you could ride with them."

"I'm not going nowhere. Not without you."

"If only we had a car. If I had some more money..."

If my Uptown relatives were here..., I think but don't say.

"This Katrina is going to be bad. But no worse than the worst storm. The hurricane isn't the bad thing. But I can't figure out what is."

I look about the house. My only home. The radio is on. The TV is loud. Mama Ya-Ya is shouting, shaking her head. Her feet are swollen in her bedroom slippers.

I sigh and say, "Spot, come." If I'm going to do this, I want company.

⁓

I climb the stairs.

I'm hoping she's not there. Hoping my mother's ghost fled the storm.

Mama Ya-Ya's room is dark. I hear wind gently rattling the windows.

I turn on the light.

On the bed is my mother. She's so light. Seems like a big wind could blow her away. She isn't solid flesh like me. Everything about her is *transparent*.

Spot walks towards the bed.

"Spot," I say.

But the silly dog is sniffing like there's no tomorrow. He goes right up to my mother's face. Her cheek is on the pillow; her eyes, open.

"Momma," I say. Twelve years and I've hardly ever spoken her name. I never told Mama Ya-Ya but I used to try and speak with her all the time. When I was a toddler, I'd crawl all over the bed, demanding her attention. From kindergarten class, I brought pictures of my hands in brown and blue paint. In second grade, I showed her how I could make an empty pop bottle sound like a flute if I blew across its top. I asked her questions about my pop, who he was, where'd he go. Sometimes, I'd get so angry 'cause she wouldn't answer. Or else, she'd just cry. Then, cry some more. After a while I stopped bothering her, just let her be. "Momma?"

Her hand reaches out as if she could pat Spot.

Spot sits, studying her.

I walk further into the room. "Momma?"

She looks like me. I'm startled. For the first time, I really see the resemblance between us — me, being twelve, and her, seventeen. There's only five years between us now. But as I've grown, she's remained the same. It helps me realize how young she was when she died. Because of me, I think. I turn to go, then, turn back. Mama Ya-Ya has never asked one thing of me. At least never something so important.

I say, "How bad is the storm going to be?"

My mother's ghost blinks. Her eyes are just as blank as the other ghosts'. Like no one is inside her body.

"How bad? Mama Ya-Ya's frightened. You remember her? You're in her bed. She helped you birth me."

Maybe I should've forgotten the birth part, since for my mother, it didn't turn out well. "I'm sorry," I say. "I don't mean to bother you. Just tell me, is the storm going to be bad?"

Spot stands, walks away. Even he sees it's a lost cause.

"Please tell me. Or if you can't talk, give me a sign."

I'm close to the bed. If my mother wore perfume, I'd smell it. Instead, there's no smell, no movement in the air surrounding her body. There is nothing in her eyes that says she knows me.

"Please," I say, bothered that I'm pleading.

My mother's ghost fades.

I'm disappointed. Even more lost than before, feeling every bit an orphan.

❧

I go downstairs. Mama Ya-Ya seems to have forgotten what she asked me to do. She's sitting in her chair, watching the TV again. The sound is off, and for some reason, it's scarier, watching the silent twirling spiral twisting on the screen, inching across the blue water, coming closer to New Orleans's shore.

Sunday

It's Sunday. EVACUATE, reads the newspaper headline. "Evacuate," say the TV anchors, looking not so pretty anymore. They look tired, a bit scared. The weatherman is no longer wearing a tie or jacket. His shirtsleeves are rolled up and he's sweating; his shirt's armpits are brown. The camera does a close-up of the weatherman's face. He says, "E-VA-CU-ATE."

I put the crocheted sofa shawl over Mama Ya-Ya. She's asleep in her favorite chair. She never went to bed.

I almost turn off the TV, but don't. Too much quiet might wake Mama Ya-Ya.

I walk through the house. Even though it's Sunday, there's no smell of cinnamon-spiced waffles or pancakes. I can't smell any bacon. (I'm not hungry anyway.)

There's quiet when there should be pots rattling in the kitchen. Me and Mama Ya-Ya should be at the table, talking up a storm. She should be telling me about signs, about how black crows are freedom birds, symbols for slaves flying back to Africa. She should be telling me how cooking black-eyed peas and greens will bring us money in the New Year. "We can always use extra," she says every time. She should be telling me why she loved me the minute she laid eyes on me — "You were special, I just knew it" — and how she has never stopped.

Spot slides up to me, his head pushing at my hand. I pet him, scratch behind his ears. "You need to go outside?" I ask, happy to have something to do.

Outside, Spot rushes to his favorite tree and pees. He sniffs every speck of dirt and every tree, happy to be outside. His tail is wagging like crazy.

I sit on the porch steps, watching the neighborhood. I don't know what to expect next. The sun is dead high in the sky.

Yesterday, some of the neighbors stopped by wanting to know what Mama Ya-Ya was going to do, believing her special powers gave her special knowledge about the storm. I told them, "Me and Mama Ya-Ya are staying put." I didn't tell them Mama Ya-Ya was *conflicted*. Another good word.

Most seemed happy that Mama Ya-Ya was going to stay.

I sit on the porch waiting for something to happen. I want to see Mary and Keisha doing double Dutch. See the men and boys staring under the hood of a car, talking about pistons and spark plugs. See Miss Leeila combing the knots out of her girls' hair and blowing kisses to her boys.

The neighborhood just seems quiet. Too quiet. The "quiet before a storm," I guess. I've read that phrase before but never knew what it meant. But now all of us, the entire neighborhood, are expecting a hurricane. Even though Katrina's still out in the Gulf. She's coming. Closer and closer.

I think quiet before the storm means it isn't really quiet. Maybe it means only now you can hear birds flying, forming a V overhead. Or that the air has sound. That it whistles, low and deep, as a storm approaches. Quiet before a storm maybe means folks are done hammering wood across their windows and placing sand sacks beside their front doors.

Or maybe it means there's loneliness. A weird loneliness that is, yet isn't, real.

⸎

I know Mama Ya-Ya says the hurricane is not the problem. But I feel scared, like bugs are crawling up and down my skin.

Mama Ya-Ya has always told me, "Some things are seen. Some are unseen. You see a lot, Lanesha.

More than most people. But life, I guarantee, will still surprise you."

I sigh. I can't see the future. Though I stare at the sky, I can't read the storm's signs.

I whistle for Spot. His big, fluffy feet tell me he's going to be a big dog.

I hug Spot, then look into his brownest eyes. "What do you see?"

His ears point straight up. He sits beside me on the porch step.

I feel nervous, watching my neighbors readying for the storm. Tonight when it hits, we'll all be inside our houses. I wonder if they feel like I do. Scared. If they worry about getting hurt or not having enough to eat. Afraid that like the big bad wolf, the wind might blow all our houses away.

❦

Other than the groceries, Mama Ya-Ya and I haven't really prepared much. I wonder if the saying "Carry an umbrella and it won't rain" might be true for hurricanes, too.

If I prepare for the worst, maybe the hurricane won't come.

Besides, that's what grown-ups are doing. Preparing.

I'm thinking Mama Ya-Ya can't afford for me to be a child no more. Since her bad dreams, she seems more a kid. Like she needs *me*.

I think of all the people Mama Ya-Ya has taken care of in her life — probably hundreds, thousands, with herbs and potions for arthritis, fevers. She's birthed babies, and when they grew up, helped birth their babies.

And there's me: 365 days × 12 years = 4,380 days that Mama Ya-Ya has cared for me. No one gave her money. Not even welfare. She could have asked but she didn't.

"Love is as love does," Mama Ya-Ya says.

So, I have to decide. Prepare or not?

Prepare.

Grow up. Time for me to make things safe — for me, Mama Ya-Ya, and Spot.

⁓

I close all the windows and get planks from the shed in the backyard. Nails, too. I pound and pound. My arms hurt and my planks aren't so great. Some are crooked and the second-story windows are boarded up from the inside, rather than the outside. But it's better than nothing.

I roast a chicken the way Mama Ya-Ya taught me. If the electricity goes, chicken will keep at room temperature. Perhaps for two days. It'll be our un-Sunday treat. Better than beans and rice. But I cook those, too. They'll take even longer to spoil. My cooking isn't as good as Mama Ya-Ya's, but I make do.

Then, I remember there's an old ice chest in the pantry. If I drag it upstairs, we can have a picnic. I rinse out the chest and fill it with ice cubes from the freezer. There's still a quart of milk and orange juice left. They'll keep cool. The chicken, too. I'm excited. I grab carrots. American cheese. There's broccoli, too, but I don't grab that.

Behind the margarine, I see a jar of applesauce. Dessert.

There's a knock on the back door. "Mama Ya-Ya, you all right?"

I open the screen door. It's Pastor Williams.

"She's fine," I say. "Please, come in." Mama Ya-Ya would want me to remember my manners.

"Lanesha, is it?"

"Yes, sir."

"We're offering comfort at the church."

"We're fine here, Pastor Williams." It's not that Mama Ya-Ya doesn't believe in God or church. She believes in many gods just as African slaves did. She says gods live in everything, in the whole wide world, so every place you are is holy.

Pastor looks at me, curiouslike. "I kept praying Delores would bring you to be baptized. She never did."

"No, sir." I am surprised that he's called Mama Ya-Ya Delores.

"Delores and I go way back. Went to school together when we were about your age. Is she all right?"

"Yes, sir. She's resting upstairs."

He blinks like an old owl. "You've got everything you need? Food? Water?"

"Yes, sir. Enough for a few days."

"Then, you ought to be just fine. Tell Delores you and she are welcome at the church."

"I will, but I don't think she'll come."

"I don't think she will either. She follows faith in her own way. It's my duty to ask. You come, if you've a mind. If the storm gets worse. More than you two can handle."

"Thank you."

Pastor Williams turned away. Then, turned back. I could tell he was struggling. Like he couldn't make up his mind whether to say something or not. Then, he did.

"I knew your mother, too, you know."

I hold my breath.

"She was a lovely girl. She wanted you very, very much."

"Did she go to your church?"

"No. But once, she visited me. You were about to be born. She said she liked the peace in my church."

I licked my lips.

"She didn't talk much." He smiled. "She said she liked the quiet, so I just sat beside her. Prayed. A few nights later, you were born. Mama Ya-Ya did let me bury her when she passed on, though. Have you visited her grave?"

I shake my head. I don't tell him that her ghost is upstairs.

"Let me know if you ever want to go. I'll take you and Mama Ya-Ya to pay your respects." He opened the screen door, stepping down the stairs.

"Where?" I say, pushing open the door.

"St. Louis Cemetery, number 2. They have a section for indigents."

The sun is three o'clock in the sky. The hurricane, says the weatherman, will arrive this evening.

Still Sunday

I gather all the candles, matches, and flashlights we have. I put them in a box in Mama Ya-Ya's room. I drag extra blankets from the linen closet and put them there, too.

Mama Ya-Ya has not left the bed today. I can tell she's trying to dream, unlock the storm's mystery. She looks terrible. She's worn the same flowery housedress for two days.

"Pastor Williams stopped by," she says. "I knew he'd come by—always does when there's trouble."

I gather my nerve and ask, "How come we never visit my momma's grave?"

"No need for that. You see her here every day."

I wince.

Mama Ya-Ya pats the bed. "Come here, precious."

I sit on the edge of the bed. I breathe her scent in deeply.

"You know dirt don't hold the dead."

"I know."

"Come, let me hold you."

I lay down and Mama Ya-Ya holds me. Spot lays his paws across our legs.

"Your momma loves you. She's so in love with you, she's never left."

"But she's not at rest."

"No. She's still trying to birth you. Wants to make sure you can survive on your own."

"Doesn't make sense."

"It will." Mama Ya-Ya squeezes me. "It will."

I lift onto my elbow and look at Mama Ya-Ya. She looks right back at me.

"You know something," I say.

"Yes, I know something. But it's not mine to tell, it's yours to figure out."

I feel irritated.

I get up. The sun is now low in the sky. I close my eyes. I can smell wet. Damp, rotting, salty wet. Katrina is coming.

❧

I can tell Mama Ya-Ya is tired.

I go downstairs to make her warm milk.

I also heat water on the stove and pour water into two hot water bottles. I place them in Mama Ya-Ya's bed and retuck her blanket.

I cook the chicken's giblets for Spot.

I lock the back screen door. I push a kitchen chair against it. I look around me—the kitchen is clean, quiet, and the refrigerator is filled with food and water.

For a minute, I feel pride. Mama Ya-Ya is still upstairs trying to dream and I have taken care of things. I'm satisfied. Content. Our house is ready for Katrina.

I step onto the porch. The sky is now orange and purple. Sundown is coming.

The air smells like barbecue. Neighbors are grilling beef and pork. I walk to the sidewalk, look left, then right. Now, everybody seems to be outside. The smells are wonderful. Hickory, brown sugar, limes. My neighborhood is partying.

Rudy waves to me. He's wearing a big chef's hat. He's cooking on the Palmers' grill. "No sense letting meat waste if the power goes out."

Mrs. Palmer shouts, "You want ribs? You and Mama Ya-Ya?"

"Yes," I say.

"I'll bring them over."

"With potato salad," says Mr. Palmer from his wheelchair.

Monique shouts, "I've got hot dogs. Want one or two?"

"Two," I answer back. One for me, one for Spot.

At this moment, I want to crush the entire neighborhood in my arms.

Rudy shouts, "Let's have salsa music."

"The Neville Brothers," says Ernestine.

"Blues," Monique hollers back.

I smile and go inside. Good thing the TV is small enough for me to lift. I carry it upstairs to Mama Ya-Ya's room.

Plugging in the TV, I tell Mama Ya-Ya all about the party. "We'll have some good food tonight. Mrs. Palmer has ribs. See, things aren't so bad. We'll be all right, tonight."

I keep talking and talking, telling Mama Ya-Ya about the food, the music, and about how happy everyone seems. How beautiful the sky looks with its orange and purple swirls.

Mama Ya-Ya doesn't say much. She can barely keep her eyes open. I don't know if she's so tired or so intent on dreaming.

* * *

I take a bubble bath. I've been saving my cherry bubbles for a special occasion. I think: What can be more special than a hurricane?

When Mama Ya-Ya gave me the bubbles last Christmas, she told me that cherries were a sign for good fortune and sweet character. "Like you, Lanesha."

When I'm finished, I just want to curl up in bed, with a soft pillow, and sleep without dreams. But I don't.

I gather up my schoolbooks, my pencils, my purple pen, and carry them to Mama Ya-Ya's bedroom. I'm almost done, ready for the night.

"Spot, do you need to go outside?" I whisper.

Spot leaps off the bed.

Mama Ya-Ya fidgets and turns in her sleep as Spot and I head outside.

❧

I see darkness on the horizon. Rolling, rolling in like a too warm blanket. Wind has picked up, blowing leaves, causing branches to sway ever so slightly.

There are covered plates by our front door. Hot dogs, ribs, and potato salad. Neighbors have shared extra food. I guess we are surviving this storm together.

The neighborhood is a ghost town. Truly. The street is darker than usual because planks and shutters across house windows keep in the light. No cars are moving down the street. No one's sitting on porches. Or walking dogs. Not even Aunt Ernestine's stray cat — the no-name cat — is anywhere to be seen. Everyone is inside, waiting.

But I see ghosts. More than I've ever seen in my entire life.

Ghosts are **LOITERING**. I like that word. STANDING IDLY, LINGERING AIMLESSLY. Me and Spot see them all. Seeing so many ghosts scares me. Before they just were — now they seem like an **OMEN**: OF BAD THINGS TO COME.

Even though I don't want to talk with them, I think now is my chance to find out what Mama Ya-Ya's dreams can't seem to tell her.

I walk to beneath the lamppost. Spot sniffs and I ask Mr. Watson's ghost, "Is the hurricane going to be bad?"

He opens his mouth and moans, "No."

A ghost girl skips rope. A ghost boy rides a bike. They smile at me.

Maybe they aren't an omen after all. Maybe they need a place, like everyone else, to see the storm through.

I pick up the food the neighbors have left. Spot licks his lips, ready for dinner. I realize I'm hungry, too. I lock the door tight and head back upstairs.

Me and Mama Ya-Ya are going to be fine. Our neighborhood is going to be fine.

∞

It's 7:00 p.m.

Mama Ya-Ya smiles weakly and sits up slowly, leaning halfway back into a pile of pillows.

I give her a spoonful of potato salad while Spot gobbles his hot dog.

"Turn on the TV, Lanesha," says Mama Ya-Ya. "Dreaming, I can't see nothin'. Hand me my glasses, honey. Let's see what the weatherman says about the storm."

Part of me doesn't want to turn on the TV. Why did I bring it upstairs anyway?

I press the power button and the screen lights up, and there he is, the sweaty weatherman.

Mama Ya-Ya sits up further. I sit beside her, a pillow behind my back. At the bottom of the bed, Spot is lying on his back, his belly up. If we were watching Oprah, we'd be having a good time.

The weatherman says, "Katrina is headed directly for New Orleans. If you haven't gotten out, buckle down. It's going to be a wild ride. Perhaps devastating."

I go to Mama Ya-Ya's window. Peek between slats. The sun's gone. The moon is yellow. The wind is whistling.

"It's coming," I hear Mama Ya-Ya say.

I shiver. Tell myself not to be afraid. We'll survive the hurricane.

Ghosts told me so.

⌁

I must've fallen asleep, because when I wake, Mama Ya-Ya has her hands thrown over her head and she is sleeping deeply. The lamp on the nightstand makes the room glow, seem unreal. Nothing's moving. No mice — they skitter at night. Not even fat water bugs that come out when you turn down the lights.

Nothing. Silence, inside and out.

I swear I can't hear a thing. No one's having a party. No fighting, laughing, singing. No words drifting up from the porches. Nothing.

The quiet makes me think I'm going to die. Like Mother Nature has sucked up everything — all sounds, winds, human talk and cries. A **VACUUM**. ABSENCE OF MATTER.

I worry I'll be sucked up, too.

But the silence doesn't last.

✑

Pop. A wild rush — a howl that is louder than anything I've ever heard before.

Mama Ya-Ya sits bolt upright.

It's the end of the world. Sounding like the explosions and screams in the D-day movies Mr. Gregg made us watch in history. It's a herd of elephants.

Wild cackling hyenas let loose. A stampede of all the jungle animals. Crackling, keening, bursting, pounding, the wind screeching like banshees. Sirens dooming sailors at sea. Rain whipping wood, *whoosh, whoosh, whoosh,* smacking at trees, beating out any sap. Like a thousand Kansas homes, not just Dorothy's, were being swept up in a tornado.

The house shakes, teetering, in the wind and rain's violent game. Dodgeball. Tug-of-war. Shakes, sways, and I swear, it's going to fall...fall, fall, fall over. Down. The bed is rattling, creeping across the floor like it grew feet.

We should all get in the tub. It is strong, tough. The bolts and pipes will hold it down. Keep us from flying, falling away.

I can't get Mama Ya-Ya out of the bed. She's too heavy for me to lift.

I scream. She screams.

I pull. "Come on," I scream. "Come on."

Her face is pale. Her bony hands are cold.

The house shudders and groans, creaks and complains like it's alive. The wind just howls back.

Her feet are on the floor; her body, slumped over. I grip her waist and pull her upright. "Please, Mama Ya-Ya, come on, please!"

She looks at me — no, through me — like she's not sure anymore who I am.

The rain sounds like someone throwing rocks at the house. Spot barks. Mama Ya-Ya jerks and I use her motion to push her forward. One step, two. Three. "Come on, you can do it," I say. I push. Pull.

Spot is rushing at the windows, barking at the wind whipping our house. Like it's a mad dog outside, trying to get in.

I scream. "Mama Ya-Ya, come on."

My face is all wet like the rain has come inside. I don't wipe my cheeks. Just keep tugging Mama Ya-Ya. My heart is about to burst.

Then, there's quiet — like the world outside has disappeared. A pocket of deep silence. It's **EERIE**. INSPIRING FEAR. DREAD.

Spot cocks his head, listening.

Mama Ya-Ya shuffles forward. Grateful, I keep hold

of her, pushing her. We make it to the bathroom and Mama Ya-Ya wants to slump down, over the toilet.

"No, here," I say, lifting her leg into the tub.

Then, *boom*. The roar is back again; stones are shattering the house. Mama Ya-Ya falls forward and I fall on top of her.

"You all right? All right?" I shriek. The rain and wind are fierce. I don't believe Mama Ya-Ya hears me even though I'm shouting in her ear. She's moaning, moaning, moaning. Is she bleeding? I grab a towel for her head.

"Spot," I scream. He hears me, and he stops snapping, growling at the monster outside, and runs, jumps into the tub.

I hug him, squeezing hard. He licks my tears. "Good dog," I say. "You're a good, good dog."

It's hot. Too humid, inside and out. I'm sweating. Hoping Spot won't leap out of the tub.

I close my eyes, getting as close as I can to Mama Ya-Ya, praying our house won't fall over. Praying she's gonna be all right.

Like a bullwhip, the rain lashes and lashes. It's getting heavier, like bricks. Smacking up, down, like a giant pounding with his fists. The world is falling apart. First, the sky, then the roof. Falling, falling, I'm sure. To crash down on our heads. We're going to die.

Mama Ya-Ya sighs like she's given up. I hug Spot even harder. We won't last the night. I hope Ginia and TaShon are safe. I hope everybody in the Superdome is safe.

The lights flicker, then it's dark. A dark deep and thick. The power is out.

I can't get to the candles or matches. I've forgotten the flashlight.

My eyes squint, getting used to the dark.

Through the door, I can see straight into Mama Ya-Ya's bedroom. Even though I've been in her room a million times, the shadows and shapes now frighten me. There are monsters here. The chair, the bed, the mirror, picking up glints of moonlight, seem to move, shuddering, trembling with spirits making them jerk, come alive.

The tub is cramped and hot.

I feel sweat trickle down my back.

"Mama Ya-Ya, you okay?"

"I'm right," she says. "I'm right."

I can't see her. Her breathing is ragged. She can't seem to get enough air. I worry. The storm is quiet, but I still listen with all my might.

Good, it's over. The storm has passed. I start to stand up but Mama Ya-Ya grabs my hand, pulling me down.

Mama Ya-Ya is holding the bathtub ledge. "Here it comes," she screams. "Here it comes."

Then, *boom*, like a bomb exploding, the storm's back.

"I-I-I-I-" Mama Ya-Ya is screaming. I scream, too. Spot howls.

Planks squeal as if they're being pulled free from nails. I hear pounding — doors flung open by wind; shutters slapping against windows; glass cracking, breaking like a thousand bottles.

"I," Mama Ya-Ya is yelling. "I."

"Eye," I realize she's saying. "We're in the hurricane's eye."

I inhale, and I try to wrap my free arm around Mama Ya-Ya. This is the worst, I think. It won't get worse. But, still, I don't think I'll make it. Wind has leaked inside. Snapping, swirling inside the house. I can feel its cool lick across my face. Pictures on the wall fall. Bedsheets billow like ghost sails. Mama Ya-Ya's Evening in Paris perfume crashes to the floor, shattering. In the cold wet, I smell dead magnolias.

How long can this last?

The tub starts to buck. Slight. Real. Its claw-feet straining up, trying to escape wood.

"Hold on," I shout. "Hold on."

Mama Ya-Ya's house is old. I'm sure the wood will snap, break. We'll fly up, towards the moon. Into the hurricane's eye. I remember a picture book with an owl, cat, and cow in a tub. We, three. We three. Spot, Mama Ya-Ya, and me will spin, cracking through the roof. Spin inside the eye.

What'll we see? What'll we see?

"Die," I holler, the word bursts out of me. "We're going to die."

The hurricane is a never-ending roller coaster.

The tub bucks again. Spot falls against me. His fur fills my mouth. Mama Ya-Ya has let go of my hand. "Mama Ya-Ya," I shout.

The tub shudders and stills. The monster is done with our house. It's moving on, raining, twisting, blowing, stomping through our neighborhood. Outside, it smashes, roars. Trees snap, metal creaks, and things—stop signs? flower boxes?—are being thrown, slapped against walls. *Thump. Thump.* I listen hard. *Retreating.* The sound is moving away like thunder that travels through the sky. The wind, no longer fierce, still blows hard. The rain snaps less like a whip.

I think I hear yelling outside: "Help me. Jesus, help me!" Cries. Is it my imagination?

Spot barks. His barks hurt my ears. I want to help. I think I should help.

What can I do? I'm scared. I climb out of the tub. "Mama Ya-Ya, I'm going to get help. Call 911."

She doesn't stop me and I try, in the heavy darkness, to press my way forward. Creeping across the tile 'til my feet touch carpet. I think this is what it feels like to be blind.

On the bed is my mother brightening, like a light. I see the phone is still on the nightstand.

I say, "Thank you, Momma," and walk towards the phone, pick it up.

I hear only silence. The line is dead.

The house is trembling again. The giant has turned back around and I no longer hear voices, hollering for help. It's too loud outside.

I think: I didn't hear anything. It was just a trick. The hurricane teasing, making me think I heard sounds that weren't there.

Then, I think I hear someone crying again. Loud, strong.

I can't stand not to know what's happening. If I can help.

We have an attic. I think if I go up there, I might hear better. See better.

See a way to help, if help is still needed.

I shiver. It's too dark. The house is rocking. I should stay put.

Then, Mama Ya-Ya shouts, "Go see. See what the storm has brought. We'll be up there soon enough." She sounds like herself again—her voice firm, steady.

I hear Spot leap from the tub and patter until his fur is beneath my fingertips. He steps slowly forward. I understand. He's guiding me. Out into the hall. We walk slowly, carefully, until my hand touches the rail, leading us to the attic door. Once we're inside, I no longer hear any voices.

There's barely any light, only moonlight that reaches through the small window.

We move slowly towards it.

I place my hands on the glass. The panes are cold, trembling.

I think the stars have all been swept away by the storm.

I stand like a big baby and cry.

Monday

It's a new day.

We have survived the storm.

Mama Ya-Ya has deep circles beneath her eyes. A big bruise and bump on her forehead. My body is sore all over.

On the bedroom window, there's a gap between planks. I press my face to the glass, peering at the morning light.

Outside, the neighborhood has been torn apart. Trees, snapped like toothpicks, are lying on the ground. A car has been turned upside down. A doormat — WELCOME — is on top of a roof. Planks dangle from windows. Doors are smashed open. A pink and yellow Big Wheel is caught on power lines, its wheels spinning. I am happy to be alive.

"Chicken," I say to Mama Ya-Ya. "We'll have chicken." Even though it is dawn, chicken seems just fine.

Mama Ya-Ya is praying before her altar, lighting rosewood incense, and picking up the statue of the Virgin Mary. Legba, who guards the spirit gates, has a broken cane. The storm damaged his head, too, and Mama Ya-Ya kisses where his hair got scraped off. Mama Ya-Ya sighs.

I think she is happy, satisfied. But when I bring the chicken (which Spot licks!), she hugs me, whispering, "The true test is coming."

I cock my head. "What d'you mean?"

"You've been so strong." Mama Ya-Ya pats my cheek and I see the clouds in her eyes. "I'm proud of you, Lanesha."

I'm proud but worried at the same time. There's more that Mama Ya-Ya isn't saying. I can feel it.

I take a deep breath and let my air out slow. I'm grumpy and I shouldn't be. We survived. Mama Ya-Ya is proud of me. All is well.

⁃⁃⁃

We sit on the bed together and eat.

Mama Ya-Ya only picks at the meat.

I think about boarding up the bedroom window. But I do not want to look outside anymore. I don't want to see the broken street. Or hear my neighbors mourning what they lost. I want to be happy—knowing me, Spot, and Mama Ya-Ya are alive.

Mama Ya-Ya leans her head back against the pillow. She says, "When I was a girl, I thought all I had to do was dream good things and they would happen. It was only later that I realized I could only 'see' the future, not control it. The truth is that even with *sight,* the world surprises you. Gives you twists and turns. Like when Charles died. When I found out I couldn't have children. When my folks and all the folks I ever knew died. When neighbors didn't want me to birth their babies anymore.

"But, you," she said, stroking my cheek, "are my sweetest gift. The life surprise that soothed all my ills and gave me my greatest joys. I feel so blessed you are mine."

"I love you, Mama Ya-Ya." I clutch her hand. I feel such calm, so lucky to be here right now. I don't ever want to live through another hurricane.

"I've been staying alive because I thought you needed me."

"Don't say that. I do need you, Mama Ya-Ya."

"No. You're strong, Lanesha. Who got us ready for the storm? Who fixed this chicken? Who looked after me when I remained in bed? Who tried to reach 911? Who tried to help?"

I set down the chicken and lay my head in her lap. I don't want to hear what Mama Ya-Ya is trying to say. I close my eyes and feel her hands smoothing my hair. Soothing me. The room smells of chicken grease, dog, Mama Ya-Ya's perfume, and Vicks. Her joints are always sore; and I'm glad she remembered to rub on the menthol from the green jar.

"I'm wearing down, honey."

I sit up and stare into Mama Ya-Ya's wrinkled face. She *is* wearing down—like a clock needing to be rewound.

"I'm eighty-two. Can't go on forever. Think I ought to stop now."

There are a million things I want to say to her. Like how much she means to me, how everything I know I learned from her, how grateful I am. But my words are choked in my throat and spill over my eyes as tears. Without Mama Ya-Ya, I will be really alone. Lonely. But I am being selfish, only thinking about me. Mama Ya-Ya is good for this world. There ought to be a law that good things and good people can't leave. Ever.

"Your turn to meet the future, precious."

Mama Ya-Ya looks like an old elf. I stroke her hand. I think what good is the future without Mama Ya-Ya?

"Eat," I say, wiping my eyes. "Let me feed you some chicken. It'll keep your strength up."

Mama Ya-Ya smiles. "That's what I say to you."

I tear off the chicken's wing. "Here. A wing, your favorite."

Mama Ya-Ya is no longer smiling. Her cheek is pressed flat against the pillow. "Time for me to pass all my remaining strength to you."

Then, she tucks herself under the covers like a child. Pulls the blankets beneath her chin. "Storm's coming," she murmurs.

"It's already been," I say.

"More," she says. Then, she opens her eyes and looks at me. Though I don't think she really sees me, just my shape in her half-blind eyes. "Do you know why your momma is still here?"

I swallow.

"She wasn't sure you were going to be all right. The world can be a hard place sometimes, Lanesha. You have to have heart. You have to be strong. Parents want their children to grow up to be strong. Not just any strong, mind you, but loving strong. Your testing should've come much, much later. But when it came, you shined with love and strength."

"You're my strength," I say, confused by Mama Ya-Ya's words. I'm not sure what I'm feeling. It's not pure happiness, but something sour. Bittersweet.

Mama Ya-Ya lifts her head, chin up. "TaShon's coming." Her gray curls flatten again on the pillow.

There's a pounding on the front door. Spot barks and runs down the stairs. I get up, glance back at Mama Ya-Ya on the bed. My mother is right beside her.

I head down the stairs.

❧

"Lanesha! Spot!" TaShon and Spot are rolling wild on the kitchen floor.

"TaShon, what're you doing here?"

"I lost my parents. There were so many people at the Superdome. I looked everywhere. You wouldn't believe it, Lanesha. Thousands of people. When the storm was over and I still didn't see them, I thought maybe they came home. So I left. When I couldn't find my parents, I came home. They're not home yet. But they will be."

TaShon seems different. When did he become so talkative? When did he get brave enough to find his way home?

"You got some milk?"

I open the refrigerator. The electricity is still off. But the milk is not yet warm. I pour TaShon a glass and watch him drink like white milk can cure anything.

TaShon is filthy and he smells like he wet the bed. But I know he is too old for bed-wetting.

"Tell me," I say.

He's still on the floor, his legs curled beneath him, his hand on Spot's fur.

"It was terrible, Lanesha. Never seen so many folks. People sleeping in the stands, on chairs, cots. Smelled real bad." TaShon wrinkles his nose. "All the bathrooms ran out of toilet paper and paper towels, real quick."

I hand TaShon another glass of milk, but he shakes his head at it. I put the glass on the counter.

"You survived the storm."

"Yeah. But it was scary. Folks shouting, crying, all the time. The storm roaring, rattling the Superdome like it weren't nothing.

"There was a big screech, Lanesha. You wouldn't believe it. A big sheet of metal was torn off the roof. Crazy! The Superdome!" TaShon looked up at the ceiling, as if it could be ripped off any second.

"Everybody went wild, Lanesha. The darkness made everything worse. You could feel the rain, thick and heavy. Hear the wind overturning cots. Hear folks screaming for their kids. But you couldn't see nothing.

"But my pop made me feel even worse. Dads aren't supposed to be scared. Pop was holding on to me. I could feel him trembling. And my pop, who ain't been to church in years, kept saying, 'Please Jesus,' and squeezing me so hard, I could barely breathe."

TaShon covers his eyes with his hands. I hug and pat his back like Mama Ya-Ya does for me when I'm scared. I kept repeating, "It's all right, TaShon. We survived."

"Even with thousands of people screaming, the wind was louder."

"I know."

"I didn't think we'd get out of there. That the wind was going to toss the Superdome like a Frisbee. Everybody inside would die."

I don't tell him about our night.

TaShon, like Mama Ya-Ya, seems to have run down. His energy drained like boys siphoning gas from a car. Sitting with his legs splayed, his head bent, and arms soft at his side, TaShon is and isn't himself.

Spot rubs his back against TaShon's thigh.

TaShon lays his head on Spot's belly. Then shivers, staring up at me. "When I couldn't find my parents, I headed for home. I figure home is our meeting place."

I see dirt, sweat, and tears dried on his face.

"They'll be home soon. I just know it."

"Sure, TaShon. Your parents will be worried, but I'm sure they'll figure out you came home."

"Where else is there to go?"

"Right, 'specially since the hurricane is gone." I pat TaShon's back again.

TaShon cries. I'm shocked. His knees are pulled up to his stomach, his head is on his knees, and he's shaking, tightening his grip about his knees, squeezing his shoulders small.

"Lanesha. I don't want to see no more. It seems even worse outside. New Orleans is all torn apart."

I want to tell him how confused I am by Mama Ya-Ya's words but, instead, I just change the subject.

"TaShon, how'd you get here?"

TaShon doesn't move.

"You couldn't have walked. Superdome is way across town."

He still doesn't move.

"Here. I can put chocolate syrup in the milk."

TaShon doesn't look up, but his nails scratch the floor. I see the stumps on his hands. TaShon, Twelve Fingers. But he didn't really have twelve fingers, just baby skin that looked like it wanted to grow. I agree with Mama Ya-Ya. It was a sign. Meaning he'd hold strong to life. I think it makes him special.

I set the glass down. "Spot needs water. You want to get it?" I hold out a bowl.

TaShon stands up. Tears have streaked his cheeks clean. He takes the bowl and turns on the faucet. Water sputters, flows yellow, then dies.

"Here. Bottled water."

TaShon pours water into the bowl, and we both stand watching Spot lap until the water's gone.

"More," I say, and TaShon pours.

When Spot's done drinking, TaShon sits on the floor beside him, his fingers tracing the linoleum cracks. He speaks softly: "I walked some. First, I thought it was fun. Like them dogs that get lost and find their way home. I climbed over all kinds of mess. Bushes. Trash. Newspaper stands knocked down. Even saw a suitcase cracked open on a telephone pole.

"Hardly anybody on the streets. I kept thinking no one was as brave as me, even though I was scared." TaShon rises to his knees, grabs his milk, and drinks it gone.

"Glass was everywhere. Cars left by the side of

the road. Even a bus got overturned. Dogs and cats everywhere, digging in trash

"Mud's everywhere. Bushes, gigantic trees pulled out of the ground. I got so I couldn't walk no more, Lanesha. It was too hot. I was tired. My legs wouldn't move. I sat on the sidewalk. A white lady with a straw hat drove by. She had a dirty-faced kid in a car seat.

"'You seen Lyle?' she asked me. I said no."

"Who's Lyle, TaShon?"

"Don't know."

"Husband, son, dog, or cat?"

TaShon shook his head. "Don't know. I asked for a ride. Said I'd help look for Lyle."

"Didn't she ask about your parents?"

"No. She kept talking about the end of the world. After a while, I told her I wanted to find my dog, Spot. She said, 'Blessed be children and animals,' and asked where I lived. 'Ninth Ward,' I said. She said she didn't think Lyle was in the Ninth Ward. But she said it wouldn't hurt to see.

"But it did, Lanesha. The porch on my house fell off. It's in the middle of the street. Momma and Pop are gonna cry. They always say, 'The house is all we have. Momma's momma left it to us.' Rudy and Rodriguez's house is a mess, too. Shutters tore off."

"Did you see them? Are they safe?"

"Don't know. Their house looks empty. Mrs. Watson's house lost its roof. I told the white lady that your house, Mama Ya-Ya's, was home."

"She just let you out?"

"Yeah. Said she had to find Lyle."

I'm still sitting on the floor. Imagining this poor lady driving and driving. I do not want to go walking in the city and see what TaShon has seen.

"Can I stay here, please, Lanesha?"

I see shadows, ghosts hiding in the kitchen corners.

I say, "Stay. Course your parents will be back. Home is home." But I'm really thinking, I'll have to take him back. Not now. But soon. If I was TaShon's mom, I'd keep looking for him until every last person left the Superdome.

Still Monday

"Mama Ya-Ya, look who's here."

"Heh, TaShon, baby. Give me some loving." Mama Ya-Ya opens her arms and TaShon throws himself into them. He holds on and Mama Ya-Ya rocks him. "Y'all eat some chicken. You're gonna need the strength."

Mama Ya-Ya sounds like her old self. Except she doesn't scold TaShon for putting his dirty self and shoes on the bed.

TaShon won't let Mama Ya-Ya go. He's hugging her hard, his hands locked behind her neck.

Mama Ya-Ya looks over his head at me, and smiles. I smile back. I know there's nothing better than Mama Ya-Ya's hugs.

"You got separated from your parents."

"Yes, ma'am."

Mama Ya-Ya holds TaShon away from her, looking straight into his eyes. "You're growing good, too. Don't worry, baby, you and your family will be all right. You'll be together soon."

"For real?"

"For real. Grab some chicken, sweetheart," Mama Ya-Ya says. "Lanesha made it. Almost as good as mine."

Mama Ya-Ya smiles. I can tell she's proud of me.

TaShon laughs. "Lanesha cooked?" He grabs the last wing and leans against the four-poster bed. Then, amazing, TaShon winks at me.

I wink back. I think the future — TaShon — will be all right.

It is still day outside. The bedroom is dark, even though there are lit candles on the altar and nightstands. Heat is rising in the room. I'm going to have to undo the boards and open the house windows. It is getting way too hot.

TaShon doesn't seem to mind. He's sitting on the floor with Spot, eating more chicken.

"What's that beside you, Mama Ya-Ya?"

"You see her?" me and Mama Ya-Ya say at the same time.

My mother's ghost seems more solid. I can see wrinkles in her nightgown. See the shape of her jaw. She has freckles like me. She is sitting up and her eyes, even though they're ghost eyes, are blinking like she's coming awake.

I step forward and my mother's ghost head turns, watching me. Can it really be like Mama Ya-Ya said? — "Everybody in Louisiana knows there be spirits walking this earth. All kinds of ghosts you can't see, not unless they want you to."

I step even closer. My mother and Mama Ya-Ya are sitting in bed like sleepover friends. Goodness.

"TaShon," Mama Ya-Ya whispers, "I'm glad you're here, honey. You're going to help Lanesha. She's going to help you."

"I know," says TaShon, biting into chicken. "You got corn?"

"No corn," I say. "You see my momma next to Mama Ya-Ya?"

"Who?" TaShon leans forward and twists. He's looking back at Mama Ya-Ya and the oversized pillows.

"Do you see her?" I almost shout.

TaShon looks at me, his eyebrows meeting in the middle of his forehead. "I don't see nothin'. Must've been a shadow. Can I have some more chicken? Please."

Mama Ya-Ya reaches out her hand. "I'm sorry, Lanesha."

"It's okay," I say, even though I'm disappointed. I hand TaShon a drumstick.

I look at my momma. She is definitely alert, watching me.

"It's grace to see both worlds, Lanesha," Mama Ya-Ya reminds me. "It's a gift." Then, she says, "TaShon, you should clean up. There's a bathroom off the hall."

Chicken grease is all over TaShon's face. "Come on, Spot." The two of them scamper off the bed and out of the bedroom.

I'm not dumb. Mama Ya-Ya got rid of TaShon on purpose.

"Lanesha, your momma and I want to help you. We've been praying. Decided we're going to help you get birthed."

"I'm already born."

"Yes. But this will be a different kind. Like a sweet sixteen. Becoming grown in a new way."

I'm shocked. My mother smiles. She's so pretty. Young. Not much older than me.

Math is supposed to explain everything but there's no equation for this. Mama Ya-Ya telling me I'm going to be born. Doesn't make sense.

"Whatever," I say, feeling too tired to argue.

"You should move to the attic, Lanesha."

"Why?"

Mama Ya-Ya takes my mother's ghostly hand. "Your momma came to me. Young and pregnant. She'd heard that I delivered babies, with no questions, no pay."

My mother is looking **ANGELIC**. An easy word: LOOKING LIKE AN ANGEL.

Mother and Mama Ya-Ya are holding hands, sitting in the bed like twins.

TaShon has come back cleaner, grinning like an idiot. He lies down on the floor, wrapping his arm about Spot, and curling up.

I speak the truth: "Mama Ya-Ya, I don't understand a word you're saying."

"It's okay. You will. The universe is shining with love, baby. To survive this night—that's what you need—love." Mama Ya-Ya reaches out both hands. "Life is full of surprises." I take her hand, feeling her palms, Mama Ya-Ya's strength.

"You need to get up to the attic," Mama Ya-Ya whispers.

"It's too hot. The hurricane is over."

"That's where you need to be," she says sternly. Then, she grimaces. "I need my medicine."

I hand her a pill and a glass of water. Mama Ya-Ya's face is gray. She takes the medicine and leans back on the pillow. My mother is gone.

❧

TaShon sleeps on the floor with Spot. Mama Ya-Ya is sleeping, too.

I take the planks off the bedroom window and open it wide. I see the damaged trees, shrubs, and houses.

The sky is beautiful after a storm. Blue. And the fresh air feels good. All the clouds have been blown into the Gulf.

I see some of the neighbors moving in the streets. They look like zombies, moving slow between damaged trees and houses. Crying at the mess. Trying to pick up and clean. Shadowing them are regular ghosts. A whole parade of them. Everyone seems to be looking for something they lost.

I feel the hair on my neck, bristling. I'm uneasy.

I look at the bed. Mama Ya-Ya is breathing heavy, though her face seems peaceful. I can't do nothing for her. Can't even call 911. I can only do what she's asked me.

I decide to move to the attic. I let TaShon sleep. I grab the water bottles, blankets, and start moving.

My mother's ghost (for the first time ever!) is out of the bed, standing at the bottom of the stairs, watching me.

I can't explain why this makes me feel so proud.

The attic is stuffy. Most areas in the attic, I have to hunch my back. I can't stand straight. Up and down the stairs I go. I lug up food. Drag up blankets. Pillows. Flashlight. Candles. Water jugs. After a while, even my momma stops standing. She sits on the stairs, watching me while I work.

I keep my mind on happy thoughts. Soon everyone will be back in Ninth Ward, making the neighborhood like it used to be. Cleaning up. I feel strange up here, making a place for us in the attic. But Mama Ya-Ya wants me to move up high, and so I do.

I grab my dictionary and the encyclopedia, Volume B, with the bridges in it.

I grab a book for TaShon.

I grab thigh meat and a bone for Spot.

If I can survive a hurricane, I can survive one night in the attic. I can do that. In a few days, I'll be at school again. Hanging out with Ginia, and sharing Spot with TaShon. He's my dog now, too.

The small attic window makes a ray of light across the floor. I look around. Everything needed is here. Then, I think, I don't know why, what if we're trapped? I won't fit through the window. It doesn't even open. I've seen pictures of folks from other storms, standing on roofs. The hurricane is gone, but what if it comes back? Can a hurricane come back?

I remember there's an axe in the shed. Be prepared and then maybe it won't happen. I think of the umbrella again — "carry it, and maybe it won't rain."

⁓

It's a sad world outside. TaShon didn't lie.

I pick my way through trash — trees downed by storm and pieces of houses, sheds' roofs ripped off. Our shed is a mess. It was never in good condition anyway, but now it looks like it's leaning and will fall down any second. I step over wood, mud, branches, sticks, carefully. The axe is usually in the back, leaning against the wall. Now it is buried beneath cans, a garden rake, and more. The shed creaks and I hold my breath, stand still — afraid I'm going to be buried. Then, I exhale, working quickly — grabbing the axe and an extra flashlight — I search for anything else that might be useful. A green tarp. I grab it and some rope. The shed creaks, shudders again.

I dash out — my heel catches on the frame. Pieces of wood, the front door, tear away and fall. I fall onto the mud. Water splashes about me.

I sit up, quick. Water? Leftover storm water, I think. But wouldn't it be soaked up by the soil?

The water seems higher. It must be my imagination. I stand quick, wiping my hands on my shirt. My jeans are wet. I squat.

There are tiny bugs floating dead in the water; others are skimming, still alive. Their tiny wings battling fierce. I think I see a leech. Slimy, fatter than a worm.

I step into the house, trying not to track water. But there's water on the floor, too. Too much water to be just from my feet.

I glance back at the door. Water is coming over the door ledge. Not much. A little. Enough. The hurricane has left. Water should be draining. Not rising.

I tremble, run upstairs to my room, and change my clothes. I do not want Mama Ya-Ya to see me so dirty or TaShon to see me so scared.

I cross the hall to Mama Ya-Ya's room. I shake her shoulder. Her eyes open.

"I'm ready," I say. "Water's coming into the house."

Mama Ya-Ya doesn't say a word. Doesn't act surprised.

"We need to get to the attic."

"Let me tell you one last story."

"There's no time."

Mama Ya-Ya ignores me. "You know how Noah, his family, and the world's animals survived the flood?"

"God sent the flood because people had been bad."

"That's the story—because people had been bad. But I tell you, Lanesha. Sometimes a storm is just a storm. A flood is just a flood."

The word *flood* bothers me.

"It doesn't matter how the flood started. What matters is how it ends."

"With a rainbow."

"Yes. All colors. All light blending beautifully. Some say it was God's promise not to send a flood again. I just focus on God's promise. It wasn't about flood, precious. Not really. It was about love."

"The universe shines down with love," I say.

"That's right." Then, Mama Ya-Ya unclasped her necklace. "Charles gave me this. Now I give it to you."

It's a gold necklace with a tiny heart that's been on Mama Ya-Ya's throat for as long as I can remember. It is delicate and strong. I put it on and it feels like a cool thread, tying me forever to Mama Ya-Ya.

"Rest now," says Mama Ya-Ya. "You're going to need your strength."

"The water is rising."

"There's time to rest," says Mama Ya-Ya. "I know some things."

True. Mama Ya-Ya knows a lot.

Besides, the room is hot. I'm tired from hauling stuff up the stairs. Just for a bit, I decide. I'll lie down just for a bit.

"Go on, baby."

I stretch out on the end of the bed, just beyond Mama Ya-Ya's feet. My hand hangs over the edge. Spot licks it, then rests his head on TaShon's thigh.

Spot is barking in the hall. Whining and barking. Running back into the bedroom, then back out again into the hall. I get up. Groggy.

I look down the stairwell and scream. Water is rising. It's halfway up the stairs. Black, nasty, swirling water.

"Mama Ya-Ya! Mama Ya-Ya, the house is flooding."

TaShon is now wide awake. Seeing the water lapping the stairs, he starts yelling. "I can't swim," he says. "I can't swim."

Spot howls.

I shake Mama Ya-Ya. She's breathing hard.

"We got to go," I scream.

Mama Ya-Ya sighs.

I want to cry. But I can't. We've got to go upstairs. "TaShon! Come on. The attic."

"I can't swim, Lanesha. I can't swim."

I scream at him, "We need to get to the attic. Help me, TaShon." I can't move Mama Ya-Ya by myself.

On the left, my arms are holding her up; TaShon is on her right. Mama Ya-Ya is heavy; her feet drag. We all stumble forward.

Mama Ya-Ya's skin is cool. Her face looks lopsided. "Come on," I say. "Try to walk, Mama Ya-Ya."

Mama Ya-Ya places her foot on the attic stair. Me and TaShon hold on. Move up, *clippity-clop*. Me, now pulling Mama Ya-Ya; TaShon, pushing.

Water is slowly climbing the stairs.

Me and TaShon slip Mama Ya-Ya into a corner in the attic. She groans.

I go back to the doorway. Look down the rickety stairs. The water has risen another step. I don't get it. The hurricane's gone. Then, I remember geography. The Mississippi. I sniff. It smells like the Mississippi. Where else would water come from? Did the hurricane make it happen? I don't know and it doesn't matter.

TaShon is crying. I turn around and shake his shoulder hard. "I need you, TaShon."

"I can't swim, Lanesha."

"Neither can I. You don't see me crying." Why cry?

I don't know too many Ninth Ward folks that can swim. No one has a pool, not even the city.

TaShon is watching me. His nose is red and his fingers are curled around Spot's collar.

"Look. The water is rising slowly. I think we'll be fine."

"What if the water gets in the attic?"

I don't think it will. But I say, "Doggy-paddle. If Spot can do it, you can, too." I show him the movements as best I remember. "Pretend you're a dog, walking like a dog, walking in the water."

TaShon moves his hands like prancing paws. "Like this?"

I nod my head yes. This seems to calm him. "We're going to be fine," I say. "Make a bed for you and Spot."

TaShon attacks the blankets and sheets. Making them float in the air before straightening them on the floor.

I sit on the floor beside Mama Ya-Ya and think about the problem. How to make sure the four of us survive? Someone will come. What if no one comes?

The water will stop rising. What if the water doesn't stop rising?

Sweat is beading on my head. It's hot. TaShon has already taken off his shirt, and Spot seems listless. I undo the buttons around Mama Ya-Ya's throat.

I hold the gallon of water to her lips. She doesn't drink. So I just wet her lips.

I pour water in my hand for Spot. TaShon drinks, too. I don't drink. The water has to last.

❧

Night isn't good. We are afraid of the dark. But the flashlights have to last. The candles, too. We can't burn them all night. So Mama Ya-Ya, TaShon, Spot, and me sit close. The room is like thick black velvet wrapped around us. My head hurts from the heat, from the musty smell.

TaShon is chattering about when his parents get home. I don't listen, just say, "Hunh-huh." Then, I hear, "I've got to go to the bathroom."

I turn on the flashlight and look at TaShon. Around our small room. There's no privacy. Or toilet or bucket. I grab a cup and hand it to him. "Use this."

"Ugh," says TaShon.

"It's all we have."

I hear TaShon making a kinda choking sound. I think he's crying. But he's laughing. I laugh a little, too.

"Here, TaShon. Take a flashlight. I'll go sit on the steps."

I close the attic door and sit down. I flash my second light down the stairs. I cover my mouth. Mama Ya-Ya's angel statues are floating, tossing, and turning in the water. Seeing them should make me sad, I think, but instead, I feel calmed. Mama Ya-Ya has told me everything is a sign. The floating statues remind me of God's promise. Tomorrow, I think, there will be rainbows. We'll be rescued. Maybe TaShon's parents will come. "The universe shines down with love," I say, repeating Mama Ya-Ya's words.

Everything is going to be okay. I might build bridges that can cross any ocean, river, or stream. I might study butterflies, how they grow from a gray-white cocoon into something colorful and beautiful. I might study words and create my own dictionary. I might do anything when I grow up.

❧

I knock on the door, poke my head in. "You okay?"

"Yeah," says TaShon. "Spot, too."

Spot is wagging his tail. Happier. The attic smells but I don't say anything. I feel dizzy. I take a swallow of water. Can't help thinking, what goes in must come out.

❧

I flash the light at Mama Ya-Ya. Sweat is draining from her face. She's too hot. There's nothing I can do. She's lying on her side, her eyes wide like she can see things that aren't there.

I want to talk with her but I'm not sure she can hear me. Or, if she can, she gives no sign.

I turn off the flashlight. One night. Just one night in the attic, I tell myself.

I don't tell TaShon the water is still rising. Instead, I ask him, "What do you want to be when you grow up?"

"A golfer."

I almost laugh. The Ninth Ward doesn't have golf courses either. No one I know has ever hit a white ball. Certainly not TaShon. "Good," I say. "I'll bet you'll be a great player one day."

"What about you, Lanesha?"

"Engineer." I think this is right. I like how the word sounds. How I could draw signs on a page that might become a bridge.

"You'll be a good engineer."

"Thanks, TaShon." We're both quiet in the dark, listening to each other breathing. It feels good to have TaShon with me.

"Were you always this normal, TaShon? I mean,

you were so quiet, I never knew. You're" — I lick my lips — "nice."

TaShon doesn't say anything. I can't see his face and I worry that he thinks I'm being mean.

"I think I'm normal," he says softly.

I can barely hear him, but I don't say anything. I keep extra quiet.

"I just figure if I keep quiet, they won't see me. Won't make fun of me for being so short."

"I thought that was the reason."

"For real?" TaShon asks, surprised.

"For real." Then, it is my turn to say softly, "Sometimes I see what others don't."

"You're like Mama Ya-Ya," says TaShon. "Special."

"Really?" I swallow hard. "I mean, you really think so, TaShon?"

"Naw. Any day of the week, boys are more special than girls."

"TaShon!"

He laughs and the sound sparkles in the hot, dark attic. I hate it when kids tease me. TaShon's teasing, though, feels good. I laugh, too.

"Lanesha, you asleep?" TaShon asks in the dark.

I wonder what time it is—eleven? Two in the morning? I feel like it's many hours before dawn. I'm tired. But I'm keeping watch. Even though I can't see nothing in the dark.

"I can't sleep."

"Here," I say. "Light this candle and read." It is a white candle in a glass jar. One of Mama Ya-Ya's altar candles.

TaShon strikes the match and I see his dirty, sweaty face. The candle makes a little circle of light.

"You should sleep, Lanesha. I'll stay awake in case Mama Ya-Ya needs anything. That's why you're awake, isn't it?"

"Yes." But Mama Ya-Ya isn't the only reason. I don't want to tell TaShon about the rising water.

"Try to sleep, Lanesha. I'll keep watch."

"That's okay, TaShon."

"No, please. I can look out for you and Mama Ya-Ya."

TaShon's words feel like a cool breeze. No one has looked out for me and Mama Ya-Ya, except me and Mama Ya-Ya.

"I'll sleep," I say. But I know I won't. *Just in case...* *just in case...* Don't think it, I tell myself. But I think it anyway. *Just in case the water keeps rising.*

"Good," says TaShon, and I can tell by his voice that he's feeling proud. "I'm on duty," he says. "Spot's second-in-command." Even though I can't see him, I know he's smiling.

In the attic, TaShon is a dark lump, with a flickering light, curled up reading. The other dark spot I know is Spot. I hear pages turning.

I keep still, letting TaShon think I'm sleeping.

I wish I could sleep. Then, I wouldn't feel I'm suffocating in the dark heat, hear Mama Ya-Ya's breathing ragged and slow, or smell the Mississippi living in our house.

I hold Mama Ya-Ya's hand—and I let myself think what I know—Mama Ya-Ya's dying.

Eight means the start of something new. Two means kindness, quiet power. Mama Ya-Ya is eighty-two. She has wound down. Her spirit is ready for something new. I smile but my heart hurts. I can imagine Mama Ya-Ya telling Mr. Death stories. Telling him that $8 + 2 = 10$. Ten means everything's complete. Perfect. Done.

I never thought I could love Mama Ya-Ya more than I already do, but somehow, in this moment, I do. I have never felt so grateful in my life.

I curl myself up, right next to Mama Ya-Ya. Her skin feels so soft and still smells sweet. My breathing matches hers. I think of how Mama Ya-Ya taught me to talk, walk, and see. How every birthday, she spent time with me, showering me with love. How every birthday, we cooked, ate cake, washed dishes, and stayed close like a real family.

I whisper in her ear: "I loved being yours, Mama Ya-Ya." I feel her squeeze my hand. "We're all in the attic." She squeezes my hand again. I kiss her fore-head. "We'll be fine," I say. "We'll be fine. Me and TaShon."

I squeeze her hand.

Part of me is glad I can't clearly see her face. That she can't clearly see mine.

I tell TaShon, "I'm awake now. You should sleep."

TaShon blows out his candle. He hasn't read a page in a while.

I can hear Spot, panting. He must be so hot.

I curl back up to Mama Ya-Ya. I don't know if she can hear me but I tell her I'm going to remember everything she taught me. I'm going to raise butter-flies, and keep looking for signs that others don't see.

I tell Mama Ya-Ya, "We're all okay." I hold her hand until her hand slips out of mine. I put my head to her chest, listening for breathing. Feeling for her lungs to rise. It's only then I cry. My hand cover-ing my mouth, though no sound is coming out. Spot comes over and licks my face. I put a blanket over Mama Ya-Ya.

I sit, in the dark, touching the necklace, feeling the love inside it heating my skin, warming my heart.

⌒⌒

As time slips by, as the water rises, I try to think about what's next, about what Mama Ya-Ya would want me to do.

8 + 4 = 12. Spiritual strength. Real strength, Lanesha. Like butterflies.

⌒⌒

I get up, tiptoe so I won't wake TaShon; I open the door, and shine the flashlight down the steps. The water is halfway up the staircase. I want to curl up and cry. But I won't. Mama Ya-Ya wouldn't want me to give up.

Solve problems. Think, Lanesha. Time. It's sometimes a variable in math.

That's it! Time. I can measure the rate of water rising over time.

I sit and count, "One, one thousand, two, one thousand, three, one thousand..." I count until my mouth cracks dry. I watch the black liquid crawling up the steps. Sixty-one one thousands equals a minute. I count six hundred minutes. That's ten minutes for the water to rise halfway up a step. Another ten to cover a new step. Twenty minutes for each whole step. There are twelve steps to the attic floor.

Twenty minutes times twelve. We've got two hours left.

Survive.

Monday Isn't Over

TaShon is snoring. Spot, too.

I shine the flashlight at the door. Water is trickling into the attic. It's a thin stream getting wider and wider.

Soon Mama Ya-Ya's body will be floating.

I don't wake TaShon.

I push, drag the highest furniture over to the window. It's in the middle of the attic, the highest point where the roof planes meet.

I stare out the window. No breeze. Or wind. The hurricane is surely gone.

Outside, I can see water, covering one-story houses, almost to their rooftops. Cars are completely covered. Lamps and electric poles look half their size. Treetops seem like bushes growing out of water.

I start, back and forth, carrying our water and food atop a tall chest. I put the pre-algebra book up high, too. The encyclopedia is too heavy. The dictionary is in my pocket. But I don't know what happened to my sparkly pens.

I shiver. I'm too hot. Sweaty. Hungry. I think I may faint.

"TaShon, get up." I shake him. Then, I move the flashlight away from his face and shine the light on the dark water coming for us. It's slipping underneath the attic door.

"We need to get higher," I say. Soon, the water will touch our feet, our bodies, our clothes.

TaShon whispers, "You think my parents are all right?"

"Sure," I say. Even though I have no idea.

TaShon grabs my arm. "Where's Mama Ya-Ya?"

"She's dead." I can't see his face. "It's all right." I

almost say, "I'll see her soon. As a ghost." But I don't. Thinking these words, I feel happier, stronger. Never before did I see any good side to seeing ghosts. But the thought of being able to see Mama Ya-Ya again comforts me.

TaShon seems stunned.

"Come on," I say. "We've got to survive."

"Wait," says TaShon.

I can't help it, but I feel irritated with him again. We need to get safe.

"Where is it?" he asks.

"What?"

"The axe."

I exhale. TaShon's right. We need the axe. I shine the flashlight over the floor. "Near the door," I shout.

TaShon runs. The axe is wet with stinky water.

"Like a hatchet," TaShon says. Then, before I can say anything, he's climbing awkwardly with the axe. With the flashlight, I shine the way. TaShon tilts, almost throws the axe on top of the high box.

"Now, let's get Spot," he says, climbing back down.

The water keeps steadily rising. Together, we climb

high on the boxes, the old furniture, trying to reach the tallest height, a flattop chifforo chest. We pass Spot between the two of us, as we climb higher and higher. There's barely enough room for the three of us atop the chifforo. The axe, thanks to TaShon, is in reach. But the food and water are on another chest, maybe three feet away. If the water rises too high, I might not be able to get to it.

I tell TaShon and Spot, "Be still. I'm going to get across to some water, food. We'll have to hold it on our lap."

"Be careful."

I try to walk across dirty tarp-covered furniture. My steps are uneven. My foot slips and a chair rattles and hits the floor. Water splashes. I grab a gallon of water and a bowl of beans and rice. I want to grab the pre-algebra book but it'll be too heavy and I don't have enough hands. Already, I have to put the flashlight in my other pocket. I can barely see.

My ankle twists and I almost fall. I hold tight to the water jug, but the beans and rice tilts and half of it falls into the stinky water below. Strange, the water seems like it's rising faster. It is maybe two, three feet high? If I was standing in it, I'm sure it would be higher than my knees.

I move more carefully. TaShon grabs my hand and I sit beside him. Sweat all over me. My shirt is sticking to my back.

"Here. Eat."

"What about you?"

"I'm all right."

"No, you've got to eat, too." TaShon holds out the plate. "Eat."

I don't have a spoon or fork. So I use my fingers.

TaShon eats, too. "Wish I had some bread."

"With butter," I say.

"To slop up the beans and rice, Lanesha. Like gravy."

We crouch like bugs on top of the chest. Our feet can't hang free — else our legs and pants will get wet. I know in an hour, our limbs will fall asleep and hurt to move. We won't last long this way.

We've got to get out of the attic. If I stood in the water, I think it would cover me past my waist.

"TaShon, hand me the axe."

"Let me," he says.

"No. I'm bigger. You know it's true."

TaShon bites his lip, then nods. "Okay." He hands me the axe.

I stand, stooping, my back curled, and swing the axe at the window. Glass breaks. The frame splinters, just a bit. There's not enough space. I can't stand tall enough and put my weight into the swing.

TaShon mutters, "We're going to drown."

"Sit down," I shout. My back hurts. I tightly grab the handle and twist my body. I hit hard. Harder and harder at the window frame. All my fear lets loose... all my hurt... even anger that Mama Ya-Ya is dead. *Bam.* The power is in my arms. I swing and swing 'til there's a ragged hole around the window. A hole big enough to climb through.

"You go first, TaShon."

"I wish I had six fingers now. I could hold on better."

"True," I say, pushing him a bit up and through the hole. I can see stars above his head. I shout, "You okay?"

"It's another world up here. Fresh air."

"Go on, Spot."

Spot scrambles through. TaShon grabs him by his furry neck. Then, it's my turn. I look back at the attic overflowing, filled with floating wood and memories. The only home I've ever known.

The moon glows high. I reach for it and escape up and out to the roof.

Tuesday

No land. Only sky and dirty water.

TaShon has his head buried in Spot's fur. He's cry-ing full-out — sobbing like the world has ended and Noah hasn't landed his ark.

I want to sit and cry, too. But it's almost dawn, and I think when there's light, someone will surely find us. I also think, still dark, I've got to make sure TaShon doesn't fall off the roof into the water.

I feel tired, sad. Even though I expect to see her

as a ghost, I know I'll still miss the flesh and blood Mama Ya-Ya. The warm hands. Her making breakfast. And me resting my head upon her shoulder. I'll miss talking to her. Listening to her stories.

TaShon lifts his head and wipes his eyes. He looks far-off. For a minute, I think he's going to be his quiet old self, and pretend to disappear. Then, he says softly, "Fortitude."

"Strength to endure."

"That's right. We're going to show fortitude."

TaShon and I scoot closer, our arms and legs touching. I put my arms around him; he puts his arms around me. Neither of us moves. I know we are both thinking, murmuring in our minds, over and over again, "Fortitude. Fortitude. Fortitude."

⁂

Sunrise. As far as my eye can see, there is water.

The Mississippi is brown, filled with leaves, branches, and pieces of folks' lives. I see a plastic three-wheeler tangled in algae. I see a picture frame with a gap-toothed boy smiling in black and white. I see a red car, a Ford, floating.

Overhead, I hear a helicopter. It sounds like a lawn mower in the sky.

Me and TaShon start yelling, waving our hands. "Here, over here." The helicopter doesn't seem to see us. It keeps flying south. Its big bird wings circling and the roar of its engine getting softer.

TaShon is cursing now. I haven't the heart to say, "Watch your mouth." I'm positive the 'copter man saw us. How come he didn't stop? Lift us in the air with rope?

I start trembling and look around my neighborhood. The horizon is like none I've seen before. Just tips of houses. Tops or halves of trees. Lampposts hacked off by water. Rooftops—some flat, some angular—most, empty.

Far left, I see a man and woman sitting on a roof, their feet in the water. Two blocks east, I see what I think is an entire family. Five, six people, all different sizes, waving white sheets. I hear them screaming, calling for help.

Where are the others? At the Superdome? Safe in Baton Rouge?

TaShon says softly, "At least we made it out of the attic, didn't we, Lanesha?"

I look at TaShon. I should've known better. Should've known that there was more to see about TaShon than he ever let show. He's a butterfly, too.

"Yes, we did," I say. "We made it out."

∽

No one is coming. All day and all night, we waited. Spot panted, slept. TaShon swatted at mosquitoes and his feet turned itchy red after he left them in the water to cool off. We are both sunburned. Funny, I didn't think black folks sunburned. But all day in the sun, no shade, has made me and TaShon red faced. My cheeks and shoulders hurt like someone touched them with a hot iron.

I keep focused on the horizon. Above it, I search for helicopters. Below it, I search for signs of my neighbors.

I used to think the Mississippi was beautiful. Not anymore. Up close, it is filled with garbage, clothes and furniture, ugly catfish and eels.

My lips are cracked. I'm hungry. Thirsty. Tired. I tell TaShon a hundred different Bible stories—all about hope. I tell him about Moses, David and Goliath, and Noah's ark. "Someone's coming," I insist. "People know we're here." But I feel Spot, if he could talk, would say, "That's a lie," then blink his big brown eyes.

❧

The moon is high. TaShon is feverish and asleep. His legs, up to his knees, are bright red. His face is peeling.

I haven't seen any ghosts either. Are they scared?

I murmur, "Mama Ya-Ya, help me. Momma, help me." But the night doesn't answer. Nothing shimmers. There's no message from another world.

❧

Day two since the flood. Day three since the hurricane.

No one has come to our rescue. There's no TV. No radio. No news from anywhere. The family that has been hollering for help is quiet now.

I can't make the Mississippi disappear. I can't make food and water appear. But we're going to go stir-crazy, get more and more miserable.

I press my head to my hand. I feel dizzy.

TaShon's itching, rubbing his left foot against his right leg. "Look. A rowboat."

I exhale. "Mr. Henri's! He liked catfish. He always gave some to Mama Ya-Ya."

TaShon's eyes are bright.

I move to the left — careful not to slip in the water, my feet angling on the roof. It's slippery. Water is in my tennis shoes. The shingles are slick with oil and gunk.

I can barely see the house next door. Most of it is covered with water. But a rowboat is floating, caught between our two houses and a bigger willow tree that kept it from floating down the street. It is maybe six, seven feet away. It's south, *perpendicular* to both our houses. "A sharp right angle." If it'd been parallel, it might've floated out — at least on the north side. But the angle kept it safe.

"Do you think we can reach it?" asks TaShon. "The boat?"

I squint. The boat's rope must be floating deep, loose inside the water.

My arms aren't long enough to push the boat free and I'm not sure I can doggy-paddle to it.

"The angle's all wrong."

Well, right and wrong, I think. Right, 'cause being perpendicular, it didn't get swept away in the storm. Wrong, 'cause being perpendicular, it needs to be unstuck.

I see TaShon's shoulders sagging. Giving up.

How can I rescue a rowboat?

EVERYTHING IS MATH. Think, Lanesha.

I look about. There are all kinds of pieces of wood, trees floating in the water. I see a long, thin trunk floating.

"TaShon. We've got to catch that tree." It looks like a young willow. Just a few years old.

I'm sure my hands can fit around its trunk. With effort, I can hold it like a stick.

I lie down on my stomach, shouting, "Come on, come on!" like a lunatic to the tree. It bobs left, then right. Then turns sideways.

"We got to grab it, TaShon!"

TaShon lies beside me on his stomach, too. We flap our hands in the water, trying to make it draw near. Trying to create another current in the muddy tide.

"It's coming," hollers TaShon. "It's coming."

"Brace yourself." Though the tree is moving slow, it'll be heavy. "Don't fall! Don't fall in."

I stretch my arms wide, clawing at the water, trying to move the trunk closer. I strain, feeling the pull in my shoulders. Water is lapping, almost to my chin.

I clutch bark. A piece cracks away in my hand.

"Get it, get it," TaShon screams. His arms are too short. The trunk is floating by.

I inch my body further, my hips and legs still touching the roof. Inhaling, I plunge forward. My arms are around the tree.

"Grab my legs, TaShon." I don't want to float down this new river.

TaShon grabs my leg, and pulls, and pulls.

If the trunk were heavier, bigger, I wouldn't be able to hold on. But as TaShon pulls me, I pull the thin trunk onto our roof. Like a seesaw, the triangle of the roof keeps it balanced, straight.

"Now what?"

"We've got to knock the boat free."

TaShon looks at me, his eyes wide. I start laughing. Can't stop. TaShon starts laughing, too.

"It's like playing pool. See. The boat is stuck; if we can knock it free, it'll float right past us."

"How do you know?"

I shrug and sigh. The sun is too hot on my neck. I want to give up. Just lie on the roof, space out, and not think about being wet, hungry.

"How do you know?" TaShon insists again.

"I don't know. But I want to. 'Sides, what else we going to do? Try or not try?"

"Try," says TaShon. Then, his nose scrunches. "I want to see my parents."

I shiver, suddenly cold. I've no one left to see. Then, I say, "I want to see Miss Johnson. Go back to school."

"I want to go back to school, too. I want ice cream."

"Bacon."

"Grits."

"Apple pie."

"Stop, Lanesha. I can't take it no more. My stomach's growling."

"Come on. Let's do it." I'm shouting like a cheerleader. "You hold the trunk's end, TaShon, and I'll try to punch the boat. Make sure you don't fall off the roof! Brace your feet strong."

I hold the trunk in my arms and pull it around like a lance. I wonder how knights moved their huge poles on horses?

The trunk wants to tilt up; I push it down with all my might. But I can't figure out how to jut it forward. There's another foot before the tree will touch the boat.

"Move forward, TaShon. We've got to get to the very edge."

We inch like baby caterpillars along the roof.

TaShon's foot slips. He stumbles. I lose balance and start to slide. The trunk hits my chin and I see stars. I taste blood in my mouth.

My feet catch on the gutters. Water splashes up to my waist. One hand holds on to the roof; the other holds the trunk, bobbing, sliding through my arm. Tilting deeper into the water.

TaShon's legs are dangling, his hands holding tight to the roof. The tree trunk is bobbing beside our roof.

"TaShon, help me," I cry. "Grab the end of the tree."

TaShon grabs the trunk with all his might. I see muscles in his arms, neck, face clench. I pull, steady myself, crawl to the roof edge, then lie on my belly, grabbing the end of the trunk. Together, me and TaShon inch the long, slim trunk out of the water, balancing it with our hands and bodies.

I think: Thank goodness, the tree trunk isn't bigger. Thank goodness, I have TaShon.

"Okay, let's try again. Rise." We both stand, the trunk in our hands, our feet angled on either side of the rooftop.

But now TaShon is in front of me, rather than behind.

"We need to change places," I say.

"I don't think I can," says TaShon, glancing back, his face strained. "I'm afraid I'll fall in. I can't swim."

Spot is behind me, panting.

"Don't you want ice cream?"

TaShon looks back at me. His arms are trembling from holding the heavy tree. He smiles. Then, face grim, he starts to inch backward.

When he's almost to my chest, I say, "Stop. I'll step around you."

"Okay." He gasps. Sweat is dripping from his shoulder blades.

I study the problem. If I let go of the trunk, TaShon will be unbalanced, unable to hold it. I need to be stronger than I've ever been. Need to be quick.

"TaShon, I'm going to let go one hand. Throw it around you and catch the trunk. You'll need to keep still. Let me circle around you. 'Kay? Okay?"

TaShon, quiet, just nods.

"I'll count to three."

"Okay."

"One. Two. Three." My hand brushes past him, clutches the trunk. TaShon is drawn tight to my chest and I hop left, wobble. Then slide my right foot towards my left, release my right hand, then reach around TaShon. The trunk tilts forwards. It's going to fall. TaShon can't hold it!

Like lightning, I grab it with both hands. I feel TaShon's breath on my neck. He dips his knees and gets a tighter grip.

The trunk is balanced between us.

"We did it," I shout.

TaShon murmurs, "I can't hold it much longer."

The trunk is maybe five feet long; it is bigger, heavier than TaShon. As big as me. "Yes, you can, TaShon. You like sundaes? I like milk shakes best."

TaShon tightens his grip. The trunk is better balanced.

"Good," I say. "Move forward. Careful. Be careful."

We inch until I am as far as I can go without my

feet being in water. We both are balanced on the roof. Spot is just behind us, studying us two. I wish Spot had hands.

"Pretend we're playing pool. We got to punch the rowboat free. Hit its back end, so the front pokes free. Ready?"

"Ready."

"One. Two. Three. Punch."

We punch with the trunk. The trunk end misses the boat, falls forward into the water.

"Lean back," I yell.

Me and TaShon lean back, offsetting the tree's drop into the water. But we counterbalance too much. The trunk points towards the clouds. We're losing our balance.

"Level," I shout. "We need to level it."

"Pull," says TaShon.

"Yes, pull." We pull the trunk back and down. Parallel to the roof.

My hands are red, scratchy. I don't dare release the trunk. I don't dare see how tired TaShon is.

I look at the rowboat bobbing. "Again," I cry. "Aim.

One. Two. Three. Punch." A hit. The boat bobs and moves forward.

TaShon yells, "We did it."

"No, we didn't." Not enough to get the rowboat unstuck.

"We can't do this," says TaShon, dropping his end of the trunk.

I almost fall backwards.

"We've got to," I say. "Mama Ya-Ya wouldn't want us to give up. Pick up the trunk, TaShon. Pick it up. I can't do this without you."

TaShon picks up the trunk.

I stare at the boat caught between houses and a tree. What if I've made a mistake? What if the rope isn't free? What if it's caught on something hiding beneath the water? What if it'll never be free?

I won't think about it.

The blue boat needs to be rocked. Unsettled. Freed from its mooring. From being trapped.

"Let's sit for a minute," I say. "Together. One. Two. Three." We sit, slowly inching our butts onto the roof, cradling the trunk against our chests and on our laps.

Spot inches forward and smells the wood. He's hoping for magic, too.

Anyone coming by would think we were crazy. A dog. Two kids sitting on a roof, just above water, holding a piece of a tree.

But that's the point. No one is coming. At least, not yet. I blink. Maybe never. Naw, I think. Then, think again, Maybe never.

I look out at the expanse of water. My neighborhood is buried as surely as my mother is buried in St. Louis Cemetery. As Mama Ya-Ya is buried inside in the water.

"TaShon, I've got to get in the water." I look at the water. It's nasty. But what choice do I have?

"You'll drown, Lanesha."

"No, I won't," I say firmly. "Together, we'll push the trunk and I'll leap at the end. Off the roof. Try to hit the rowboat. Use my body's motion to set it free.

"Let's stand." I start standing, feeling TaShon rising with me, wobbling a bit.

"We need to do this, TaShon. I'll say, 'One. Two. Three. Push.' Got it?" I don't look back to see if

TaShon agrees. I somehow know that he won't disappoint me. We'll be a team.

I scream, "*One, two, three! Push!*"

We push, a huge effort, and I run right off the roof, and splash in the dirty water.

I hold my breath, grunt as I push. Then, I sink down. Down into a darkness darker than night. Darker than the attic without lights.

My eyes sting. I kick. Hard.

I cough out the awful water and try to swim. Try to knock the boat free with the trunk. Me and TaShon have got the boat's tip facing more north. Angling into the water, instead of towards the house.

I am strong. Not scared. I think this in a blink of a butterfly's eye.

I think: Pretend the water is land. Water is heavy. It'll hold me. "Run, Lanesha," I scream, and I can't hear anything except water lapping in my ears and I push with all my might.

The boat moves, rocks against the house and tree. It tips more north. I scream again, and it's me, pushing the tree trunk into the boat.

The boat bobbles, side to side. Up and down. Then, it's free. The current moving the blue rowboat, bobbing it towards me.

"Yes." I pump my arms. "Yes."

"Yes," TaShon echoes.

I kick my legs, pull water back with my arms, and I'm swimming, like a dog, not caring about the things touching my legs, bumping into me.

"Help!" Something has grabbed me. A branch, a twisted scarf, I don't know. My right leg is stuck, being pulled down, beneath the water. My hands flail and splash, trying to keep my head above water. My head is tipped back, parallel to the sky. I'm panicking. Puckering like a fish.

Wood hits my chin. Scrapes against my ears. It hurts bad. I'm tired. Way too tired. I don't know why I thought I could solve things. Give up, Lanesha, I think. Just give up. Soon as I think it, I become weak like a baby. I hear TaShon yelling for me. Spot barking, crazy wild.

But I sink slowly into the muddy, pitch-black water. The Mississippi is making me a new home.

My clothes and shoes are getting heavier and heavier. My head can't stay above water. I flail my arms, and kick.

In the water, which used to be my street, it's like a new country. I can't see stop signs, fences, or sidewalks that I know must be there. I make myself close my burning eyes—I can't see anyway!

Then, I think: Fight, Lanesha. I kick, flap my arms, but I don't move up. Something—I don't know what—is still holding me. I try not to think what it might be—a tree branch, slimy algae, wood, or something dead.

It's quiet in the dark. I can't hear TaShon or Spot, just water rushing against and in and out of my ears. The water feels more and more like a thick stew. I'm confused. Where's up? I kick. My lungs ache. I'm going nowhere.

Then, I feel a kiss. I open my eyes. My mother is shining—a bright, radiant light, and I can see. See her long black hair, brown skin, and lips that seem pink with lipstick. But it's her eyes that make all the difference. They aren't dull and blank. They're seeing me.

"*Lanesha.*" It sounds like bells when she says it. The second syllable is bright and crisp. Not like Mama Ya-Ya who calls my name, drawing out the third syllable, the *ah* sound.

"*La-nee-sha.*" I feel good inside. She has been waiting all this time to say my name; I have been waiting just as long to hear it.

My mother points. I'm caught in a tree's thick branch. She floats down, like crystal light, and untangles me from the branch. My legs are free. At first, tired, I slip deeper, but then I hear my mother say: "*Pull, Lanesha. Pull.*"

I am not too tired.

My arms reach, my feet kick. My mother boosts me from below. I fly like a rocket. I pull strong, slapping away driftwood, fallen leaves, pulling, pushing the muddy water down.

My hand touches the boat. The wood feels good and I pull myself into the boat, collapsing onto the planks. I feel the boat floating, rocking me. On my back, I catch my breath, my chest rising and falling, and see blue sky and clouds shaped like huge pancakes.

I prop myself up onto my elbow. "TaShon."

TaShon whoops, hollers.

I look around. Peer over the boat edge. My mother is gone. I can't see any light, only the dark water.

"Lanesha, Lanesha! I thought you were gone."

"I wouldn't leave you." My mother didn't leave me, I think, but don't say.

The oars are under the seat. I grab them and put them in the paddle holder. I pull and the boat dips to the right. I pull some more — not caring that I'm dirty and my eyes still sting. There are some weird bites on my arms and legs. My shoulders hurt. I pull the oars back, lifting up water, splashing it down.

I row until the boat is further north, between our two houses, nearer to where our street becomes a stream.

"Jump, TaShon." It isn't too, too far from the roof to the boat. But far enough.

TaShon flies. I press my butt into the boat to keep it stable. I reach and catch skinny TaShon. He holds on to me for dear life. Me, him.

"Mama Ya-Ya would be proud of us," I say.

TaShon sighs, happily sitting on the rowboat bench. He bobs his head, calling, "Spot. Here, boy."

Spot paces. Whimpers.

"Come on, boy," I shout.

"Please, Spot. Good, good dog," hollers TaShon.

Pacing back and forth, tip to tip, end to end, on the roof, Spot's scared. His tail is drooping. He doesn't like this Mississippi water. This small blue boat.

"Come on. Come on, boy."

Spot sits and my heart sinks for I think he has decided not to move. Then, he leaps, lifts off his haunches, and flies. Right into me and TaShon's arms. The boat rocks. Water rushes in. I think we're going to topple over. But we don't.

We all hug. Spot licks our faces, never minding the wet muck on mine. TaShon is crying, not caring that I can see.

I row. It's harder than it looks. I row, wanting to make TaShon happy. Happier.

I wish I could see Mama Ya-Ya. Hear her laugh and clap her hands at all I've done. At all me and TaShon have done to help ourselves.

I see a bright ripple, like lightning, in the water. It's Mama Ya-Ya's ghost rising, all sparkly like diamonds, all glittering with rainbows.

"Mama Ya-Ya?"

"She here?" TaShon looks around. "Don't see nothin'."

I feel alone again with my gift. Crazy Lanesha. Except, I'm not.

"Lanesha, you're one sweet child," says Mama Ya-Ya.

Tears fill my eyes.

"You're going to be fine, Lanesha." Then, I see my momma, softly shining beside Mama Ya-Ya. Together, they both say, "We love you," and I feel such peace coming over me. Happiness, like a light inside me, breaking into a million pieces.

"Lanesha, let's get out of here," says TaShon. "Let's find water. Food."

‿◦‿

Both my mothers are fading. Then, gone. Yet not. They'll always be together and always be with me.

I think: How lucky I am to see the dead.

How my neighborhood seems dead. Yet not.

❦

I'm so happy. The boat is big enough for us. One dog.
Two kids.

We lift the oars out of the water and rest.

❦

I look at TaShon. Behind him, over his head, I see
the sun. To the left, what was left of Mama Ya-Ya's
house. Now, there's just clouds. And in the water,
two tops of trees.

"We have to row, TaShon. Until we see a bridge.
An overpass. Something to climb up on. Above the
water. Ready?"

TaShon bites his lip.

"Mama Ya-Ya says we're going to be fine, TaShon. I
say, we're going to be best friends forever."

He nods.

"Ready?"

"Ready."

My voice strong, I shout, "One. Two. Three."

We row. Both of our hands on one oar. Straining to move the oars through thick water, then lift the oars up, then down. Again and again. Water splashes. Through water, up and down, we try to row.

The boat rocks, confused. We even manage to turn ourselves around. The boat points, for a moment, out to sea.

"Stop," I say.

"It hurts," says TaShon.

"I know." A dead rat bumps against our boat. Neither me nor TaShon scream.

"We've got to keep even, row together. Ready?"

"Ready." Surprising me, TaShon starts singing! He sings: "Row, row, row your boat."

I laugh.

"Come on, Lanesha. Row, row, row —"

"— row your boat. Gently down the stream."

Together, we sing-shout: "Merrily, merrily, merrily, merrily, life is but a dream."

We keep pace together. Us both rowing, stretching our backs, our legs. Pushing against the current with all the strength we've got.

"You sound like a frog," I say to TaShon.

He laughs full-out. My laughter matches his, starting in my belly and bubbling out.

What is it that makes laughter feel so good? I think I must remember this moment. When I am in trouble again, when life surprises me, I should laugh.

Thirsty, sore, sunburned, blisters bubbling on our hands, laughing, me and TaShon are having fun.

We hear helicopters, but we don't look up. If they drop a rope, then we'll catch it. Otherwise, we keep singing. Keep rowing.

"Merrily, merrily, merrily, merrily..." This is my favorite part. We are merry. In our world, in our boat. As new friends.

In my mind, I see triangles. The boat angling towards land, not sea.

Ghosts are all on the left, near the sea.

Spot's ears are perked high. He sees them, too. TaShon doesn't.

I keep singing. I sense, if they could, the dead would build a bridge. Help the living. If their spirits were concrete, we, and the rest of the Ninth Ward (all of New Orleans), would be forever safe. Ghost levees. Ghost bridges.

"There!" I scream. "There." It's the Martin Luther King Bridge overpass. It's more beautiful than the Golden Gate. Rising up and over the water. I see tons of people on it, walking. To where, I don't know. To someplace safe. That I know. Someplace safer than the flooded Ninth Ward.

❧

"Look, Lanesha."

I hear it, before I see it. A motorboat, with two men with shotguns, putters behind us. "Are you kids all right?"

"We're fine," I say.

"Hungry. Thirsty," says TaShon.

The men—good Cajun folk—give us a jug of water and PowerBars.

"Do you know anyone else that need rescuing?"

Inside, I feel good. Me and TaShon have rescued ourselves. With my hand, I shade my eyes. "There's a family miles back," I say. "In our neighborhood. Ninth Ward."

"Rescue boats should be getting over there soon."

"Great," I say.

"'Bout time," says TaShon.

The man with his belly folding over his belt asks, "Where's your parents?"

"At the Superdome," says TaShon before I can speak.

"Your parents are going to be proud of you," says the potbellied man. Then, both men tip their straw hats like me and TaShon are grown-ups.

I lift the oars. "Bye, misters."

"Thank you," says TaShon, all polite.

"You two deserve an escort." The second man ties a rope to our boat. "Ready?"

Me and TaShon grin. Pull our oars in.

The motorboat jerks forward. The engine *put-putters.*

I relax, lying back, my hands crossed behind my head. I love the blue sky. I feel like I can do anything. Like I'm butterfly strong.

TaShon is waving at the folks on the bridge. All of them are shouting, waving at us.

Bruises are all over me. I stink. I'm wet. I'm happy.

I search the sky for rainbows. I don't see any. But I know it doesn't mean they're not there.

⁂

I've been born to a new life. I don't know what's going to happen to me.

I just know I'm going to be all right.

I'm Lanesha. Born with a caul. Interpreter of symbols and signs. Future engineer. Shining love.

I'm Lanesha.

I'm Mama Ya-Ya's girl.

A Note from the Author

Dear readers,

Hurricanes are like whirling, water-filled tornadoes. Warm ocean waters are spun by equatorial winds and a vortex is created. This mass of heat and wind can move quickly with a frightening energy, often causing damage once it hits land.

On August 28, 2005, Hurricane Katrina was declared a category 5 hurricane with winds up to 175 miles per hour and surging water up to twenty-eight feet high and hundreds of miles wide. Directly in its path was New Orleans, Louisiana.

The massive storm surges flooded property and tore buildings from their foundations. Though severely damaged, New Orleans survived the hurricane. But the surging water had also destroyed many of the storm walls and levees (embankments intended to hold back rising water) that had been erected specifically to protect the city, because it had been built below sea level. As water continued to breach the walls and levees, the bowl-shaped city flooded, causing even more destruction.

Hurricane Katrina was a casualty experienced by many Gulf Coast communities from Florida to Alabama to Mississippi to Louisiana. Nearly 1,800 people died, thousands were injured, many were left homeless, and property damage was estimated to be in the tens of billions of dollars

The lower Ninth Ward was one of the most devastated New Orleans communities.

The residents of New Orleans, with help from people around the world, continue their efforts to rebuild and restore this beloved historic city.

Sincerely,
Jewell